THE WILD CHIHUAHUAS OF MEXICO

THE AMAZING TALE OF HOW A PACK OF WILD CHIHUAHUAS HELPED WIN THE MEXICAN REVOLUTION

Tampico Press Books
Pasadena, California
Tampicopressbooks.com

Although this book is based on facts and historical accounts of the Mexican Revolution, it is a work of fiction and many names, characters, places, and incidents are the product of the author's imagination.

Gomez Rhine, Traude
The Wild Chihuahuas of Mexico by Traude Gomez Rhine
Summary: A pack of wild Chihuahuas, lead by alpha dog Lola, journeys across the Chihuahuan Desert in search of Pancho Villa during the Mexican Revolution. Along the way the dogs learn important lessons about leadership.
1. Dogs-Fiction. 2. Chihuahuas-Fiction. 3. Mexico-Fiction. 4. Mexican Revolution-Fiction. 5. Pancho Villa-Fiction.

ISBN-10: 0989919404
ISBN-13: 978-0-9899194-0-1

Designed by Hortensia Chu
Cover illustration by Michael C. Rhine

THE WILD CHIHUAHUAS OF MEXICO

Traude Gomez Rhine

Tampico
PRESS BOOKS

FOREWORD

This story springs from the little-known fact that many years ago small, wild dogs roamed through the deserts of Chihuahua, Mexico.

Chihuahua, the largest of Mexico's thirty-one states, is famous for many things. The spectacular Copper Canyon in the Sierra Madre Mountains, for example, is a geological wonder that rivals Arizona's Grand Canyon. Chihuahua is also famous as the home of Mexico's revolutionary leader Francisco "Pancho" Villa. During the Mexican Revolution of 1910 to 1920, Pancho Villa fought against the Mexican government in the country's north while his *compadre* Emiliano Zapata fought in the south. Both revolutionaries wanted to empower Mexican *campesinos*, forced to work for little money on the *haciendas* of the wealthy landowners. In fact, a fascinating bit of history involves the Sierra Madre Mountains, Pancho Villa, and a pack of wild Chihuahuas.

By now you may be shaking your head, saying that Chihuahuas are tiny dogs with mighty personalities, often pampered by their owners and even dressed in silly outfits. What could these yapping lapdogs possibly have to do with the Sierra Madre Mountains and Pancho Villa? Read this book and you will find out. Once you finish, you may say this story is too far-fetched and there is no way of knowing if it is true.

I can only say, there is no way of knowing that it's not.

Traude Gomez Rhine

ONE

April 1916

Chihuahua, Mexico

Ten small dogs gathered on the cliff and stared down at the village that lay in the valley beneath them. With her eagle eyes, Lola, the leader of the pack, watched puffs of smoke rising from chimneys atop several of the small adobe huts. A swirl of colorful activity danced before her eyes. The villagers were busy this morning; women hung laundry on clotheslines and swept courtyards, and groups of children were running around playing. Chickens clucked in the courtyards and a donkey tied to a fence post brayed. Poor and simple, this village looked just like the last one the dogs had raided, but this time Lola felt sure they would make off like bandits. The dogs would not be beaten back with sticks and brooms.

"Those villagers won't know what happened when we charge in running and barking," Lola told the other dogs who huddled around her. "They'll rue the day that we took them by storm."

Lola suddenly caught a whiff of something that made her sit up straighter. She sniffed the breeze and the wonderful smell of fresh salty pork filled her nose. Someone had recently killed a pig. She quickly scanned the village below, almost frantic; on a wood fence that ran alongside of one hut, she spotted a string of sausages dangling from a post. Lola's sharp eyes zeroed in like a circling hawk's on a mouse. The hunger that she had tried to ignore came roaring back to life. Her mouth began to water.

"We'll be lucky today," Lola said, but she kept her discovery quiet so that she could surprise the pack later. "We'll find plenty of meat and eat until our bellies are round and fat."

She puffed out her chest and tried to look brave for the other dogs, whose tails drooped between their legs, and whose sharp rib bones poked through their matted fur.

What a sorry bunch, Lola thought. *So hungry and beaten down from too many days of not enough food.* Her black whiskers twitched as they always did when she was nervous. *I'll get those sausages if it's the last thing I do.*

"You'd better not take us on another wild-goose chase," grunted Joaquín, a dusty black Chihuahua with long spindly legs. His rough gray tongue hung from his mouth, parched from the heat like an old piece of leather.

"Chili's looking really bad," Joaquín continued. "I'm surprised he's still alive. He needs more to eat than the scrawny lizards we've come across. We didn't find any food in that last village raid, just got chased by angry people with sticks. You'd better make this raid work or the dogs will suffer even more."

Lola glanced at poor Chili. The old gray Chihuahua had been with the pack longer than Lola herself, even longer than her *padre*. His short legs wobbled and his sad face slumped against his grizzled chest. A fly buzzed about his head as if it sensed he would soon fall over. Lola swallowed hard. Joaquín was right; Chili looked terrible.

"I'm okay, Lola," Chili said, trying to stand taller on his trembling legs. "This raid will be a success; I feel it in my bones. Lead the way and I'll bite the ankle of any foot that tries to stop us from getting meat."

Lola couldn't bear to let Chili down, but she was not at all sure the dogs could scare the villagers and steal the meat as they had once so bravely done. Mexico's legendary Chihuahua raids— with hundreds of dogs overrunning villages, baring their dangerous teeth, and frightening everyone in sight—were over. Lola remembered running beside her *padre* in one such exciting raid just outside of Chihuahua City. It was a story the villagers would tell around their campfires for years to come—hundreds of frenzied, attacking Chihuahuas! The dogs made off with a dozen roasted chickens that they gobbled up beneath a full moon.

What a fiesta they had, howling along with the coyotes until daybreak. Lola decided that night that she would someday lead the pack, even though she was a girl. Her *padre*, Cuauhtémoc, had said that she could do it, that she was brave and smart and strong.

But now the pack was smaller than ever—no longer hundreds of dogs strong, it numbered less than one hundred, less than fifty. Just ten miserable, starved, and half-mad dogs remained. Three dogs had been lost in the past week alone. Two had simply wandered away and one died from the blazing heat and starvation. Chili's cousin Don Diego had just fallen over in the dirt and was instantly swarmed by flies.

Lola and Dolores helped Chili bury Don Diego in the shallow grave he sadly dug with his paws, but the other dogs had trotted on as they could not bear to watch.

Worse than the pack's small size was its gloomy mood. Times were hard for the wild Chihuahuas. Some villages were nearly empty as so many men had gone off to fight with the great revolutionary leader Pancho Villa. It seemed that all those who remained were practically starving—the old men, the women and children, the dogs and donkeys, the iguanas and lizards; everyone and everything left behind was skinny and scrawny.

But the good times were coming back; Lola could feel it in her bones. If only the dogs could stick it out a little longer. Surely the fighting would soon stop, the men would return, and the villages would be filled with food once again.

"Chili, stay here and we'll bring back meat," Lola said calmly, though her heart was beating as fast as a butterfly's wings. "Keep Dolores company."

Lola nodded toward the pack's oldest dog, the fragile but regal Dolores, whose long once-glamorous red fur was covered with burrs. Even as the dogs limped through the dusty desert, Dolores held her head high as if she were a royal dog who belonged in an ancient Aztec temple. Lola knew about the Aztec kings and their royal dogs because sometimes at night Dolores told the dogs stories about these special Chihuahuas who lived among the ancient Aztecs. Lola marveled that Dolores knew so much about these people and their special dogs who had vanished from Mexico six centuries before.

"So sorry to be such trouble. It used to be me who ran in front of the pack, when I was young and strong . . ." Chili's voice trailed off, and his sad head hung even lower.

"You were certainly among the bravest of dogs," Dolores said, her warm brown eyes filled with kindness. "But we've had our glory, Chili. Let's leave the raiding to the young dogs, and us old dogs shall rest beneath the cactus."

"Lola won't let us down," Chili said as he collapsed in the dirt. "And after I have a little food and get some rest I'll feel good as new. I'll join you on the next raid, Lola. Just you wait and see."

"This will be a great raid," Lola said, though she knew her words sounded hollow. Still, those dangling sausages were a good omen—a good omen, indeed.

Joaquín shook his head. "I'll believe it when I see it," he sneered.

With that, before Joaquín could say another word, Lola took off running down the hill. She would never let Joaquín steal her pack. Never.

"Run, run," she barked at the other dogs trailing behind her. "We're fierce, we're proud, we're the wild Chihuahuas of Mexico!"

The dogs swarmed down the road leading to the village barking their war cries as if they themselves were a band of Aztec warriors.

"Better watch out because here I come," barked Bombom, a fuzzy white Chihuahua with a patch of black fur circling one eye. Intensely loyal, Bombom was always just inches from Lola's side.

"I'm going to steal all your stinkin' food," barked Pedro, Bombom's cousin who was all black with a white patch around his eye. Pedro could not resist using the word "stinkin'" in every sentence he uttered.

As the dogs burst into the *zócalo*, a clutch of women scattered into their huts.

With the dogs causing a ruckus and distracting the villagers, Lola began scouting for her treasure. Her nose led the way, hot on the scent of the salty pork. She ran along the village's narrow dirt paths, sending chickens squawking and jumping out of her way. She passed the bored-looking donkey tied to a post.

"We're the wild Chihuahuas of Mexico!" she barked.

The donkey hardly blinked an eye and swatted at some flies with his tail.

Suit yourself, Lola thought, annoyed that the donkey had not been impressed. There was a time when the village animals would cheer as the dogs ran through. The Chihuahuas never harmed another animal; that was a cardinal rule.

Lola rounded a corner and came upon the fence she had spied from the hillside. The long string of sausages hung down, glistening in the sunlight. Her heart soared. The strand was longer than she had thought. She quickly counted—twelve sausages, one for each dog and then some! She had saved the pack! Lola's tail began wagging furiously with great relief.

Lola jumped up to snatch the sausages but she fell back to the ground with a thump, her teeth clattering and her mouth still empty.

"Yiyiyi!" she yelped. The fence was higher than she had figured. Lola's head began to spin. She would just have to jump higher. She lowered her body to the ground and focused on the prize.

You can do it! she told herself. *You're Lola, the bravest, strongest, and smartest Chihuahua this side of the Sierra Madres.*

At that moment, from the corner of her eye, Lola spied an old woman charging toward her with a broom.

"You'll be sorry, you disgusting desert rat," the old woman screamed, her long silver braid flipping around her head. "Wild dogs are not tolerated! Neither are bandits!"

Holy tamale! The old *abuelas* were the meanest. They would gladly kill a dog, throw it in the pot with the chicken, and then cackle with the other *abuelas* sitting round the fire. Lola had seconds to reach those sausages. She jumped, missed again, and came down even harder. Her skinny legs buckled. *I'm too weak from not eating.* She was seized by panic as it hit her that she might not get the sausages after all.

The old woman was by now whirling about and smacking her broom in all directions, a furious tornado. Lola knew she had time for one last jump—one last chance to get the sausages, to save her Chihuahuas, to be a hero.

"I am Lola, leader of the wild Chihuahuas of Mexico," she barked.

And with every last ounce of energy, as if her life depended on her strength, because it did, Lola jumped at the dangling sausages.

Dear Virgin of Guadalupe, help me, she prayed in midair. *Save my dogs.*

Her jaw sunk into something soft and salty. Her body hung in space, suspended, as if she were just one more sausage on the row.

The old woman was so close Lola could smell her sour odor, the powerful mix of tobacco, onions, and *copal,* with a heavy dose of sweat. Lola paddled her legs in space. She kicked against the fence. The old woman was howling now like a hyena, displaying a full set of blackened teeth, coming in for the kill.

Down Lola fell. She hit the ground in the shadow of the broom as the old woman aimed for her head. But Lola ran like the wind. She wanted to warn the other dogs to run away but she could not risk dropping the sausages. With luck, the other dogs had taken what they could get and were headed back up the hill.

On the way out of the village, she passed Donkey once again.

"Go, little dog!" he brayed, swishing his tail back and forth and grinning wide to display a row of perfect white teeth.

TWO

Lola sped away from the village, her jaws clamped down tight on the sausages.

I won't drop them, I won't, she thought as she ran along a trail carved into the hillside by the countless villagers who had walked along it for hundreds of years. Lola's heart pounded against her chest, but it was not fear that drove her along. It was pure excitement that set her tiny feet running faster and faster.

I showed that nasty abuela, *that* loca *old lady,* she thought, delighting in her daring escapade.

As Lola ran, she kicked up red dirt that covered the mountain and it settled upon her light tan coat. Streaked with brown and black, her fur was a patchwork that reflected all the colors of the desert, from the lightest shade of sand to the blackest night.

Lola's black eyes shone, her black nose and black whiskers twitched.

Lola was a strong dog, medium-sized for a Chihuahua, with sleek muscles and a broad chest. She was not a pretty dog but she was handsome and admired by many.

Lola was so excited and bursting with confidence that she decided to leave the path and run through a field of wild blue agave. She loved dodging among the spiky plants that grew in thick clusters. The sausages did not weigh as much as she had imagined they would, and she picked up speed, running faster and faster, her white paws barely touching the ground.

Suddenly, Lola was not running alone; suddenly, she was running alongside her *padre,* Cuauhtémoc, the bravest Chihuahua she had ever known. Cuauhtémoc, named for the courageous Aztec ruler of Tenochtitlan, the capital city of the Aztec Empire that once stretched across Mexico, was the fastest, smartest, and most beloved of all the Chihuahuas. When Cuauhtémoc first led the pack, the dogs ate well because the villages were still filled with men and food and her *padre* knew how to get what they needed.

Cuauhtémoc used to tell Lola of the time before the Revolution started, six years earlier, when some people had not only tolerated but even loved the wild dogs and would throw them old chicken and goat bones. When Lola was born four years ago, the Revolution was just beginning its second year, and in every year since, as the fighting raged on, the villages became emptier and the dogs grew skinnier. More and more, the villagers kept their chicken and goat bones for themselves.

Lola ran and ran, swept up in the memory of her *padre*. If only Cuauhtémoc could see her now with all these sausages, wouldn't he be proud? More than anything, Lola wanted to be a powerful leader like her *padre*; she wished it so badly, she could almost hear her father's voice saying that it was so.

Lola suddenly remembered her pack: Pepe, Manny, Mela, Nini, Pedro, Bombom, Dolores, Chili, and even Joaquín, all looking to her to protect them. Lola began to tremble from nose to tail. No, Cuauhtémoc would not be singing Lola's praises—he would be horrified to see how far the pack had fallen in the year since his death.

Lola then thought of another leader whose courage she wanted as her own: Pancho Villa, who was as great a leader to the people of Northern Mexico as Cuauhtémoc had been to the dogs. Lola knew this by the way the villagers and Indians chanted his name and by the songs they sang of his courage. Why, just the other day, she had heard two men talking of Villa when she snuck into their village late at night to steal the tortillas that had fallen beside their fire pit.

"Pancho Villa can command his men to ride on horseback all night on empty stomachs, then attack the *Federales* at dawn and win!" said one, twirling his thick black mustache with busy fingers.

"That's why we call him Centaur of the North—he's half-man, half-horse," said the other. "Such an excellent horseman has never ridden across the desert."

"He's destroyed the *haciendas* of those *hacendados* who stole our land and who forced us to grow their corn and make them rich with our hard labor," said the first. "He's the fastest horseman and the greatest gunfighter in all of Mexico, fearless in the face of danger. He's a born leader."

"*Ya viene*! Here he comes now!" shouted the other man, laughing and pointing into the night. "Villa, Friend of the Poor!"

Both men nodded and raised their hands to the sky. "*Viva* Pancho Villa," they cried. "*Viva* Mexico!"

A born leader! The idea made Lola soar over the ground. How wonderful to be born under such a powerful star.

It's not too late, Lola thought, running with a fresh burst of energy and resolve. *I can still be a great leader and make the pack strong again. If Pancho Villa can lift up the villagers, I can make the Chihuahuas strong too. Call me Pancho Lola*! Lola wanted to bark these words to the world but she did not dare loosen her grasp on the sausages.

Just then, the sharp arm of an agave poked Lola's side, deflating her dream and sending panic and worry flooding back through her body.

How much longer could Lola really expect her scared and starving dogs to follow her? What if Joaquín convinced them that he should take her place?

Wait until they see these sausages, Lola thought. *That'll make them happy, even if just for a little while.*

With panting breath, Lola reached the hilltop where the dogs had now regrouped. She dropped her head, opened her mouth, and let the sausages fall to the ground. She looked straight up into Joaquín's furious, snapping black eyes.

"A disaster, an absolute disaster," he growled.

"What?" Lola was eager to point out the wonderful row of plump, juicy, salty sausages, but before she had a chance, the other Chihuahuas crowded around her, snarling and pushing. Pepe was the first to dive for a sausage but the others quickly followed, tearing in to the links with brutal force.

"Stop, stop," Lola barked. "There's plenty for everyone! Chili and Dolores must eat first."

"There's not enough stinkin' food!" raged Pedro.

"Give it to me!" barked Mela.

"I'm going to eat it all!" whined Pepe.

"It's mine!" barked Nini.

The dogs were growling and lunging at each other, for they were starving and as desperate as they had ever been.

"Stop fighting," Lola barked. "I brought back food for everyone!"

Joaquín growled deeply, "A couple of torn-up sausages? That's going to feed the pack?"

"What?" Lola searched the ground for the long line of plump sausages but the dogs had already gobbled up whatever there was.

How could they eat twelve sausages so quickly?

A sickening feeling filled Lola's empty stomach. Had she only managed to pull two sausages off the fence? She had not had time to notice once she hit the ground. Or had the sausages broken off as Lola ran through the agave field, lost in her own dreams and memories?

What happened to all the sausages?

Several other dogs crowded around and began to whimper.

"We didn't get anything, not even a bite," said Bombom.

"But didn't anyone else find anything?"

"Pedro found a few old tortillas," Bombom said wistfully. "They look like leftovers from the mice."

"Stinkin' tortillas," Pedro whined.

"Why did you risk our lives to raid a village with hardly any food?" demanded Joaquín, circling Lola with hunched shoulders and bared teeth. Joaquín's black eyes seemed to burn and spit out sparks from between his narrowed lids.

The moment had finally arrived. Joaquín had needed an excuse to challenge Lola to a fight, and now he had one. As Joaquín circled and growled, the fur on Lola's back began to rise. She turned to face her nemesis. Lola hunched her shoulders and bared her teeth as well; her growls and snarls were just as savage as Joaquín's. The other dogs drew in close.

"Go, Joaquín," barked Pepe.

What! Pepe was siding with Joaquín? Lola turned and snapped at him.

"Go, Lola," barked Bombom.

Joaquín struck first, pouncing on Lola and knocking her to the ground. He sunk his teeth into Lola's neck; the pure hatred flowing from Joaquín felt like snake venom shooting into her blood.

Filled with fury, Lola jumped up and bit Joaquín's backside. Suddenly, the dogs were locked in a vicious roll, legs and tails tangled, teeth snapping, fur flying.

A single thought ricocheted through Lola's head as she tumbled on the ground: *I'll fight Joaquín to the death so he can never challenge me again.*

But then Lola heard a voice that made her stop. A frantic, anxious voice cut through the calamity.

"Stop, please stop! It's Chili, poor Chili."

Lola and Joaquín stopped in mid-fight. They turned to face Dolores who was hovering beside them.

"Get away, old dog!" barked Joaquín, his black eyes still spitting out sparks. "You'll get hurt as I take Lola down."

"What, Dolores, is Chili sick? Is he hurt?" Lola broke away from Joaquín's grip, panting hard. He had bitten her shoulder badly and she winced in pain.

Dolores shook her head and sank to the ground. "Not sick, not hurt."

"What then?"

"I do believe he's dead."

THREE

The dogs ran over to Chili, and there he lay in the dirt. Poor Chili. His eyes were closed, and he looked to be sleeping peacefully, except no one would be sleeping peacefully lying out in the middle of the day with the hot sun beating down. He lay absolutely still. His chest did not rise and fall; he was not breathing.

Old Chili. Apart from Dolores, he was the last of the older Chihuahuas who had run as young dogs with Cuauhtémoc, and he was dead in the dirt, his body already swarmed by flies. The unbearable heat brought the flies out thicker than mosquitoes.

After Cuauhtémoc died, it was Chili and Dolores who comforted Lola when she missed her father so badly that she sometimes whimpered half the night. It was Chili and Dolores who had sided with Lola when she fought to lead the pack, even though some dogs judged her too young and, worse than that, unfit because she was a girl. A girl had never, ever led the pack and some Chihuahuas were furious at Lola for her ambition.

But Lola had beaten every male contender fair and square, and in the end, after suffering some bloody wounds, she had won her place.

Lola knew that Chili had always seen the best parts of Cuauhtémoc within her.

"You are indeed Cuauhtémoc's daughter," Chili told her many times. "You have the same daring spirit and courage."

Now, Lola shook on her trembling legs. If only she had brought all the sausages back, maybe she could have saved Chili.

"Chili's heart was as big as a bull's," Dolores said softly, her head drooping just inches from where his gigantic heart, no longer beating, lay under his patchy gray fur. The sight of his ribs through his sparse coat broke her heart.

Why did Chili have to suffer so when he had never hurt anyone his entire life?

Lola began digging in the dirt as fast as she could without taking a rest until she'd dug a hole. She then used her mouth to drag Chili's small body into the grave. She kicked dirt over Chili until he was hidden from sight. It wasn't much of a grave but perhaps it would keep away vultures, if even for a few days.

"Come on," Joaquín said when Lola had finished. He was wearing what Lola could only regard as a smirk of satisfaction. "See what happens to dogs who run with this pack? If you want to be the next Chili, stay here with Lola. But if you'd rather fill your bellies and not fall over dead in the dirt, then follow me and we will find food, I promise. We'll return to our glory days."

Several of the dogs obediently trotted over to Joaquín's side. Pepe nosed his way to the front of the group.

"Let's go," Pepe said, panting like crazy and wagging his bushy tail. Lola stiffened. Pepe and Lola had once been best buddies, wrestling together as puppies, napping side by side. In the past, Pepe had often been at Lola's side when they raided villages, howling with excitement.

Joaquín headed out into the desert, and Pedro, Pepe, and Manny followed him, without a glance back.

Lola's heart began to pound so loud it filled her ears with a terrible banging; she had just lost Chili and now she was about to lose half of her pack in one fell swoop.

"Wait!" she barked.

The dogs turned back at her sharp tone. A scowl darkened Joaquín's face.

Lola searched for a reason, any reason that would convince the dogs not to go. Losing these dogs meant the end of the greatest pack of Chihuahuas that had roamed the deserts of northern Mexico for many, many years, and for more than a decade with the legendary Cuauhtémoc as their leader. Her *abuela* and *abuelo* had been part of this pack, and their parents before them.

How could Lola call herself a good leader when in the past year the pack had almost completely fallen apart?

In the long silence, as Lola grasped for words, Mela meekly began walking toward Joaquín, her tail between her legs.

Dolores and Bombom huddled together and watched Lola expectantly, waiting for her to do something that could reverse this terrible situation and save the pack. If she did not, they knew, the dogs would die divided.

Help me. Someone, tell me what to do, Lola silently prayed, feeling more alone than she ever had before. *What would Cuauhtémoc do? What would Pancho Villa do?*

His head hanging, Nini began to follow the dogs now walking off into the desert. Joaquín had won over all the dogs except for Dolores and Bombom. With victory at hand, Joaquín broke into a lope, and the other dogs hurried along in his dust. In a few moments, they would pass behind a crop of rocks and be gone forever.

I'm sorry Padre, I did the best I could. Guess I just wasn't born a great leader like you after all. Lola's vision began to blur. She looked over at Dolores, who was gazing at Chili's grave.

Suddenly, a coyote scampered into view, kicking up the fine red dust as he shouted out a startling message, "Pancho Villa is dead! Pancho Villa is dead!"

His words blasted through the silence like a gunshot.

"What's that you say?" Lola barked. Her world turned over one more time.

"Pancho Villa, famous leader of the Revolution, is dead," Coyote called out without stopping. He ran even faster, as if to get away from this awful news.

"No," Lola said. "It can't be true!"

"What will happen to Mexico?" barked Mela, who, upon hearing this news, had turned away from Joaquín's group to run over to Lola. "Who will help bring meat and happiness back to the villages if not Pancho Villa?"

Just then, a black crow soared overhead, casting a shadow upon the dry earth.

"It's not true," Crow called out as he drifted down closer to the dogs. "Don't listen to Coyote. Pancho Villa is not dead. Pancho Villa is alive!"

"What do you mean? How do you know?" Lola barked into the cloudless sky. "Tell me, Crow, how you know?"

"I was flying through the Sierra Madres, and I saw Pancho Villa. He's living deep in a hill, in a dark and hidden place," Crow cawed. "I saw him stumble from a mouth in the hill, shouting to the gods, shaking his fists in anger. You may ask, was this ghost or man? I'd say man!"

"But why is Pancho Villa hiding in a cave when he's meant to fight the hero's fight?"

"He needs help," Crow cawed back. "His heart is pink with weakness and his leg is soaked with crimson blood. Black serpents dance in his head and confuse his thoughts. Who will help Pancho Villa escape the dancing serpents before they eat his entire brain?"

And with those urgent words falling through the air, Crow soared high into the sky, higher and higher until he seemed to brush the sun with his shiny black wings.

The rest of the dogs who had followed Joaquín had by now turned around and run back to Lola, yapping in excitement.

Was Pancho Villa dead, or was he living in a cave with evil black serpents twisting around his brain?

"Forget about it," growled Joaquín, running back and pushing his nose into the mix of dogs. "He's dead. You can't trust Crow to tell the truth. He's full of trickery. Anyway, who cares if some *hombre loco* is dead or alive? Come on, let's go!"

But the dogs around him now looked unsure. Mela began inching her way back toward Lola.

"No, it's Coyote who's filled with trickery," Lola said, her heart racing with this unbelievable news. It was true that coyotes had a long history of teasing and tricking the Chihuahuas, as if they were the cats and the Chihuahuas the mice. Lola knew Coyote was not to be trusted.

Her mind began racing, faster and faster. Her black whiskers quivered and her black eyes flashed. A secret wish that Lola had kept buried deep in her heart throughout this long, difficult year began to surface. Indeed, Crow's message released her pent-up desire to meet Pancho Villa. Without knowing exactly why till now, Lola had wanted this more than anything else in the world. She wanted to smell his scent and hold it deep in her nose. And Lola wanted to feel his strength, just as her *padre* had, because, she now understood that if anyone could help her to become a better leader and save the pack of wild Chihuahuas, it was Pancho Villa.

But if Pancho Villa now had a weak, pink heart, bloodied leg, and dancing serpents in his head, how could he possibly help the Chihuahuas? How could he possibly save Mexico?

Lola noticed the dogs awaiting her response to the surprising turn of events that had foiled Joaquín's plan to steal the pack.

"Some of you know that my *padre* once met Pancho Villa," Lola told the dogs gathered around.

"He did?" asked Nini, who had never actually met Cuauhtémoc but had heard many stories of his legend.

Dolores nodded, looking about at all the dogs. "Chili and I were there too."

"What happened, Lola?" asked Mela.

"Six years ago, just as the Revolution began, my *padre* took the pack to raid the village of El Apache," Lola explained. "Dolores and Chili were the only dogs from the pack still here . . . I mean, Dolores is."

"Chili was always right by Cuauhtémoc's side," said Dolores. "Chili was the most loyal *compadre* anyone could have."

"My *padre* didn't realize he was raiding a village where Pancho Villa was sleeping the night," Lola continued. "But he caught the strong smell of goat jerky and followed it through the village until it brought him to a hut. The door was open and the scent of goat jerky pulled him in. But the moment my *padre* walked through the door, someone slammed it shut behind him."

"No!" barked Nini.

"Yes!" said Lola. "And then someone then threw a *sombrero* over him."

Cuauhtémoc trapped beneath a *sombrero*! The dogs all shuddered at the thought.

"A moment later, though, the *sombrero* was lifted, and a rough hand grabbed Cuauhtémoc by his scruff and shook him around like a dancing skeleton," Lola said.

"Who shook him?" asked Mela.

"It was Pancho Villa's goat jerky that my *padre* smelled," said Lola, "and it was Pancho Villa now dangling Cuauhtémoc above a heap of jerky, laughing like a *loco hombre*."

"I will never forget what happened next," said Dolores, her brown eyes shining. "The minute the door slammed behind Cuauhtémoc, Chili took charge, and began barking to all the dogs, 'Circle the hut and prepare to fight. We're not leaving until Cuauhtémoc is freed!' So the dogs surrounded the hut and began howling. Some of Pancho Villa's men tried to chase us away, but we wouldn't stop howling, barking, and biting. And Chili howled the longest, barked the loudest, and bit the hardest."

"You'd think Pancho Villa would be furious," said Lola. "But instead, he told my *padre*, 'Your dogs are fighting for you, biting the ankles of my men, who could easily kick them from here to Cuernavaca. You must be a great leader to inspire such ferocious loyalty. I will release you back to your dogs.'"

But there was more to the story that Lola would not share. She did not tell the dogs what Cuauhtémoc told her in private and she never would. Only Lola and Cuauhtémoc and Pancho Villa would know that before Pancho Villa threw Cuauhtémoc back out the door, he cradled Lola's *padre* in his huge, rough hands.

Cuauhtémoc had never felt such strong hands, and Pancho Villa's massive power seemed to flow through his fingers right into Cuauhtémoc's fur, through his skin, and into his blood.

Cuauhtémoc had never looked directly into a human's face, and Pancho Villa's hypnotic brown eyes transfixed him. As Pancho Villa gazed into Cuauhtémoc eyes, brown eyes meeting black, the dog recognized that Pancho Villa was a great leader too. Cuauhtémoc could tell by the way Pancho Villa looked straight into his eyes.

Lola noticed the dogs were all gaping at her, waiting to hear more of Cuauhtémoc's capture.

"Pancho Villa gave the dogs his entire heap of goat jerky," Lola told them, realizing the moment she said this how cruel it would sound to dogs who had nothing.

"I want some stinkin' goat jerky," whined Pedro.

"Pancho Villa told us then that he loved the little dogs," said Dolores. "He told us that packs of wild dogs ran through the deserts of Durango, where he lived as a boy, and he loved to watch them travel across the land."

As Dolores spoke, Lola became lost in her own thoughts. *If Pancho Villa were to pick me up and cradle me in his massive hands, perhaps his power would seep through my fur, and I too would become a powerful leader and could help the dogs become strong again.*

Suddenly, the fur on Lola's back stood straight up. "We must find Pancho Villa," she declared.

"What? What are you saying?" The dogs began to yap and yammer at once.

"We must find him for two reasons," Lola continued. "If Pancho Villa is in trouble, we should try to help him. And maybe, just maybe, Pancho Villa can help the Chihuahuas."

"Why should we help him," said Joaquín with a terrible, angry snarl, his mean eyes snapping. "This is the craziest talk I've ever heard. I'm the leader now, remember?" He roughly commanded the other dogs: "Let's get out of here."

Joaquín turned and trotted off into the desert. First, only Pedro and Manny followed his lead as the others held back, staring at Lola with wide eyes, but then they too turned and followed. The sun by now was high in the sky and a slight, hot breeze blew across the sand. Lola's throat was dry and her eyes burned as she watched most of her pack leave.

"Wait one minute! This is the moment of destiny that the ancient Chihuahuas, the noble Techichis, portended when they lived among the Aztecs!"

The voice rang out into the desert clear as a bell. The dogs all spun toward it in surprise.

"What? Who said that?" Several dogs ran back, calling out these questions.

"I recognize this moment—I've been awaiting this for a long, long time, perhaps for my entire life." Great excitement colored Dolores's words as she darted about. "How amazing that the story that my mother has told me since I was a little pup is now unfolding before us. It's a miracle, an absolute miracle."

But the real miracle was the transformation of Dolores from half dead to bursting with life.

A few more dogs following Joaquín came back. "What do you mean," said Pepe, whose squat little legs were so short his belly almost dragged on the ground.

Old Dolores now danced about. All the dogs came over and stared, mesmerized by her strange mood and her strange words, which jumped from her mouth like grasshoppers.

"My *abuela* first told me the story of a pack of lost and confused dogs wandering in the desert," she said. "It came to her from her grandmother and then from hers before her, and so on for hundreds of years, the story spinning around through this desert from one dog to the next. That's why stories are so important. They carry messages."

"What else did the story say?" asked Nini.

"It said that two great leaders would meet and change the course of history. This is exactly what they meant, and we must now listen. I feel it in my bones."

By now Dolores was positively acting as if her tail were on fire, spinning and jumping about. "Come back," she called to the Chihuahuas who were still standing off at a distance.

"Why should we, old dog?" barked Joaquín, his eyes blazing. "Old Dolores is mad," he told the other dogs. "Wait a minute and she'll fall over dead, just like that dead Chili. The monsters that come just before death have seized her addled brain. Maybe black serpents are dancing through her head too."

But the dogs were too stunned by Dolores's behavior to do anything but stand and stare.

"My *abuela* warned me about Crow," Dolores said, paying no attention to Joaquín. "She said, 'Beware the crow when it flies into the sun as the dogs wander the desert. Turn back and follow your true leader.'"

Dolores rushed over to Lola and stood by her side. "Chili and I knew when Lola was young that she held the power to save the dogs. It's your duty to turn around and follow Lola. Chili knew this. I feel him now; he's with us. He can't cross over until we do the right thing."

At that exact moment a wind swirled around them, kicking up the sand. Several dogs began yapping at the air.

"Chili can't leave and become a star in the sky until you turn around," Dolores barked.

"It's true, it's Chili, and he's mad," said Bombom, his ears back, looking as if he had seen a ghost because perhaps he had.

"Stop it, you insane old dog," Joaquín growled. In a rush of anger, Joaquín ran up to Dolores and knocked her to one side.

"Leave her alone!" Lola ran to Joaquín and pushed her nose into his face, angry with herself for allowing him to bully her at all.

"Dolores is our elder and we must show our respect. Now, whether Dolores has seen a vision or not, I know in my heart that it's our duty to find Pancho Villa. My *padre*, Cuauhtémoc, called Villa a great leader. Crow said Villa needed help. What if we could help him? Wouldn't we be helping all of Mexico?"

Manny nodded his head. "Maybe it's true," he said to the dogs. "Maybe Dolores isn't crazy. Maybe Chili is sending us a message." Manny stood taller with this idea. "I know I want to do something more than wander the desert looking for food, trying to stay alive for one more miserable day."

A few other dogs began to nod, inspired by the building excitement. "I think my mother also told me the story of the crow against the sun bringing a message," Bombom said. "I can't remember for sure, but it's possible."

"It sounds familiar," Pepe agreed. "I think we should go with Lola."

"Me too," said Mela.

"Me too," echoed Nini.

"Have you all lost your senses? We're leaving and we're leaving now, and if you don't come, you'll be dead in the desert in less than a week. I guarantee it." Joaquín began dashing away again but he slowed when he realized no one was following.

Lola's heart surged. She had her dogs back. "*Viva* Pancho Villa," she barked into the desert air. She began to run through the sand with Dolores on one side and Bombom on the other. She turned to see all the dogs were following her.

"*Viva* Pancho Villa," the dogs all barked back.

FOUR

Lola ran through the desert; she ran and ran. The Chihuahuas were with her, all around her, and she felt happier than she had in a long time. When was the last time she had run and barked with pure excitement, not worry and dread, bubbling in her heart? Before her lay the majestic Sierra Madre Mountains. They stretched before her like a slumbering bear, his fat tummy turned up to the sun, his arms and legs splayed about.

"We're going to the Sierra Madres to find Pancho Villa!" she barked to the world.

Then something happened; the longer Lola stared at the Sierra Madres the more her bubbling excitement sputtered and collapsed into worry and dread. She began to realize just what she had promised the dogs—a long journey. The Sierra Madres, the Mother of Mountain Ranges, was far, far away.

Lola's resolve faltered. The dogs had been running at full speed for so long the mountains, she thought, should have begun to appear bigger. But the slumbering bear was exactly the same size.

The dry and dusty desert that spread out between the dogs and the mountains was as wide as the blue sky above.

The dryness filled Lola's mouth, nose, and ears. She slowed her run. She glanced over to see Dolores panting and gasping, not really running, but sort of stumbling forward as if she would tumble over at any moment. Her eyes bulged from her head. Old Dolores, who had puffed up with conviction about the dogs' destiny, determined that they take this journey, looked like she was about to join Chili.

"Walk," Lola commanded. The dogs slowed and stopped.

"Water," Nini barked.

"Yes, water," Mela barked.

Thirst and hunger ran with the dogs. They could run fast as the wind but they could never outrun thirst and hunger. Lola could smell and feel Joaquín's gross, disgusting breath on her back. She turned to find him glaring at her.

"Oh, Great Leader, we can't go any farther without water. Why, Dolores looks like she's about to faint!"

Curses! she thought. *Why does Joaquín have to come too?*

Because he would die alone in the desert, taken by a wolf or a coyote in no time. These canine cousins didn't bother the packs so much, but a single dog was fair game. Lola had once seen a coyote's swift attack. Her whiskers twitched at the memory.

Dolores lay down on the ground, her eyes cloudy. "I'm fine, just need a short rest," she whispered. But Dolores wasn't fine. She needed water more than she needed rest. She closed her eyes.

Lola glanced around the vast desert. She did not see a single village. There was not a source of water anywhere.

But wait . . . what was that? From the corner of her eye, Lola noticed some movement on the horizon.

"Oh, Great Leader, your followers are suffering," Joaquín smirked. "Look!" Several other drooping dogs had fallen over in the dust; their eyes cloudy too.

Again, something caught Lola's eye—a strange swirl of dust. She squinted into the distance. The swirl died down, and picked up again. Then her heart warmed with relief—a miracle by the name of Chili. Lola felt certain that the dead dog was leading her somewhere.

"This way," she barked.

"The dogs are tired and thirsty," Joaquín growled. Lola growled back and the fur on her back bristled. *What's this dog's problem?* She would have to put Joaquín in his place when the time was right. He would be a thorn in her paw until she did.

Then the swirl of dust came into view again.

"Let's go," Lola barked. "Not much farther and we'll rest."

Lola ran to Dolores, still lying on her side. "Can you make it?"

Dolores opened one eye. "Chili's come to help," she whispered. "I believe I can."

Lola's eyes grew big. So Dolores knew of Chili's presence as well.

One by one the dogs rose and followed Lola as she walked in the direction of the swirl. The day had worn out by now, and the sun began its dip to the west.

Lola knew that if a great god from above looked down on the dry, wide desert and saw this tired, thirsty, beaten pack of Chihuahuas trudging through the dust, he might rub his hands together and expect the dogs to soon walk into his kingdom, for the desert could be cruel.

The desert took what she wanted with no mercy. As the dogs continued, Lola passed a few piles of bleached bones. She knew the sad fate of these animals, be it another dog, a coyote, or a rat. First they became tired and thirsty, then, overwhelmed by exhaustion, they lay down, never to stand again. The vultures came soon after; at least they ate well. The sun burned away what the vultures left until only these piles of bleached bones remained.

But just as the desert could be cruel and unforgiving, a never-ending graveyard, it could also reveal great, wonderful surprises.

The swirl rose up and as it did Lola spied the best surprise of all—a glint of blue, the most beautiful color to grace the desert. She moved along faster. Then she saw that beneath a towering ocotillo cactus, with its woody, whiplike branches angling out, there bubbled a spring, a natural pool of water that somehow rose from deep within the earth and surface at this very spot.

"Come on!" Lola called.

The dogs, sensing her excitement, lifted their heads and began running along past a cluster of agave *lechuguilla*, being careful to avoid the plants' tough and spiky leaves.

"Yi, Santa Maria, a miracle," hailed Mela when she saw the spring. Lola went to the water's edge first and took a slow, careful drink, so cool, wet, and wonderfully refreshing. She then turned and nodded at Dolores, who walked to the edge and took her own careful drink. Lola's heart burst with joy to see Dolores standing on the edge, sipping the water. The old dog looked gratefully at Lola, and a sparkle began to shine once again in her eyes.

When Dolores finally finished, Lola gave the rest of the dogs the signal, and they fell upon the spring with wagging tails, lapping the cool water with desperate tongues. After the dogs stopped drinking, Lola noticed a few dogs looking at her with awe.

"How did you know this spring lay beneath the ocotillo?" Bombom asked.

"Yeah," chimed in Pedro. "You saved our stinkin' lives!"

Lola just shook her head. She would not tell the dogs about Chili hovering above them, not just yet.

Lola then noticed Joaquín's glowering, hate-filled stare. Though he too drank his fill from the spring, he was furious that Lola had found it and given the dogs a good reason to stick by her side.

The dogs could not get enough of the cool water. A few waded into the shallow spring and they splashed and howled and played like puppies.

"This is the best day of my life," barked Mela, the one dog who could always find the best in everything. She shook her pure white coat so that droplets sprayed on everyone.

The dogs were so exhausted from the eventful day, which had started with the raid on the village and ended with the group gathered around the spring, that they wanted only to sleep. Some curled up together in the narrow shade of the ocotillo. A few found vacant holes dug by other desert animals and they burrowed into the cooler sand below ground. Then they settled down for the long, undisturbed *siesta* that they all deserved.

The sleeping dogs snored, and twitched, and yelped, dreaming so many different dreams. Bombom dreamed of eating heaps of tender goat meat. Joaquín dreamed of fighting Lola, of bloodying her fur and scratching her eyes and nose, and winning the brutal battle. Dolores dreamed of when she and Chili were puppies, of licking his face with her gentle tongue and telling him he was the best friend she had ever had.

Lola, however, dreamed of standing beside Pancho Villa on a mountainside overlooking Mexico's beautiful valleys, and Pancho Villa telling Lola she was bravest dog he had ever met. Lola did not know why she wanted Pancho Villa to tell her she was a courageous dog, but the idea made her heart sing.

The pack slept through the warm night, lulled by a faint breeze. Lola, however, woke to the sound of coyotes howling in the distance. As she loped among the dogs, making sure nothing was close enough to threaten them, she found Dolores sitting and gazing toward the charcoal sky, where a million stars twinkled.

"Why are you awake, Dolores?"

"My old bones ache on the hard ground," Dolores replied quietly. "Lola, look into the sky. You know that each star burns with the soul of an old dog, and that Chili belongs up in the sky with the thousands of dog souls that will twinkle for eternity and even longer. My *madre* and *padre* twinkle above, and my *abuela* and *abuelo* too. All the dogs that have run through the desert of Mexico since time began have made their way to the stars."

"I know, Dolores," Lola said, though she did not tell her that not once since Cuauhtémoc's death had she been able to find his star in the sky, even though she had looked and looked, and that it made her feel sad.

"Someday soon I'll be a star too, Lola. But tonight I can think only of Chili," Dolores said. "I'll make sure you cross over and find your star," she whispered as she stared into the twinkling. "Good old Chili, you won't be stranded in the in-between forever."

FIVE

The dogs woke up early, their stomachs rumbling worse than ever. Except for the few small bites of sausage the morning before, they had had nothing to eat for several days. Slowly they rose from their sleeping spots and returned to the spring to drink more water. After drinking their fill, they began sniffing around, searching for any possible morsel that could ease the biting pangs of hunger. Short of dirt and rocks, the dogs were ready to eat anything.

Pepe found some crickets beside the spring and he ingested them in a flash, barely chewing their crunchy bodies.

"Give one to me," Mela whined, but Pepe only turned and growled.

Nini had better luck. He found a dead iguana beneath an agave, not dead so long that it had completely turned to leather, but dead long enough that a dog had to chew for several moments to get one satisfying mouthful.

Nini was the sort of dog who wanted everyone to be his friend, so he gladly let all the dogs take a turn gnawing at the iguana's scaly body, even though it meant much less food for him.

Lola, meanwhile, woke ready for action, her ears and nose alert, looking, waiting, and scouting for some real meat. Something had to be alive somewhere, especially near a water source. She trotted around the spring, her nose held high. Lola had an exceptional nose. She could distinguish as many as twelve odors at once, picking one layer of smell over another; right now she smelled the iguana, the water, the crickets, and the dogs.

Wait . . . what was that?

Lola ran out into the desert. Her nose led her this way, then that, following a faint scent that rose and fell with the wind. She knew it was out there and that patience would win. Finally, she simply stopped and waited, still as a stone, but sniffing, slowly sniffing.

It came in a flash; the scent filled her nose and then the mouse scurried by. What was he thinking, that mouse, scurrying so close to Lola that she nearly pounced on top of him before he even knew what had happened.

The mouse had a moment when freedom might have been his, but confusion trapped him. Instead of running as fast as possible in one direction, he turned and stopped and turned again. Lola pounced again and the mouse was hers. She had breakfast.

Lola threw the mouse onto the dirt and walked back to where the dogs had gathered. She ignored all the dogs except one.

"Come, Dolores, you need to eat."

Dolores obediently followed Lola into the desert to share the morning's delight. She was almost crazy with hunger and the mouse's flesh was the taste of life. The other dogs watched, not daring to defy their leader's right to choose with whom she'd share her catch.

Joaquín paced back and forth as Lola and Dolores ate, never glancing in their direction. But Lola knew Joaquín was watching them with the eyes he seemed to have on the back of his head.

"I am glad we all had something to eat. I know it wasn't much, but I am sure Pancho Villa will feed us. He will share his dried goat meat and tortillas," Lola told the dogs as they huddled around. "We'd better keep moving so that we can soon reach the mountains."

"Perhaps we could stay here by the spring for a few days, and enjoy the stinkin' water," Pedro said, his big eyes filled with hope.

Lola sat up straight. "Pancho Villa is waiting. He needs our help now. We must hurry on. Quick, enjoy one last drink and off we go."

"Pancho Villa, Pancho Villa," Joaquín droned. "You'd better be right about him, little girl." But even Joaquín, his belly in knots from having nothing more than a bite of sun-baked iguana meat, was tempted to believe that Pancho Villa might have a cave full of dried goat meat that he would happily share with the Chihuahuas.

The dogs took turns lapping at the spring, and then off they ran, following Lola who headed toward the mountains. As Lola led the pack, she suddenly saw something that almost made her fall over.

A line of horse tracks stretched before her on the ground. She hoped and prayed it was a sign of luck—a good omen for the dogs.

The dogs ran for a short time before falling into a brisk, steady walk. Lola knew that she had the dogs' good mood for just a short time. The effects of the few bites of iguana, the crickets, and the bellies full of sloshing water would soon wear off. Finding food was the real work of the day.

Lola thought again of what she had seen and she still could not believe that the other dogs had not. How could they miss this important clue, especially Joaquín, who she knew, despite his bad moods, was a smart and observant dog.

The horse tracks could mean a number of things. Perhaps it was a band of Villa revolutionaries running through the desert. Even if Pancho Villa was hiding in the mountains, his men were still fighting against the *Federales*.

Or maybe the horse tracks belonged to someone who lived nearby. The thought made Lola's heart race. A village, or even a house, meant food. Finding more horse tracks could perhaps lead the dogs straight to real food. She searched the desert ground, her mind filled with one thought—horse tracks, horse tracks, horse tracks.

SIX

The dogs continued onward the slumbering bear, the Sierra Madre Mountains, where they expected to find Pancho Villa hiding in a cave.

"I'm going to run fastest so that he'll feed me first," said Bombom, trotting along beside Manny.

"No, I'll get the first piece of Pancho Villa's stinkin' goat jerky," said Pedro, hurrying up from behind.

Lola knew that many of the dogs could only imagine that wonderful moment of tasting the delicious jerky. They didn't understand the difficult journey they would endure before Pancho Villa could even offer a morsel—if the dogs could even find Pancho Villa, that is.

They would find Pancho Villa. Lola shook off the doubt and refused to let it cloud her thoughts.

In truth, the dogs had never actually been in the Sierra Madre Mountains. They had lived on the desert floor their entire lives. It had never occurred to them to travel up into the mountains, just as it had never occurred to them that they should travel to the moon. Lola knew, though, that the journey would take many long days. She knew that along the way the dogs might meet wolves, foxes, boars, and other unfriendly animals who would happily snack on a Chihuahua.

While the dogs discussed Pancho Villa and his goat jerky, Lola searched the dry ground. Her ears, eyes, and nose were in high alert, and she sensed an electric charge in the air that ruffled her fur. Through the bottoms of her paws, she began to feel a vibration. She recognized it as the power of a group of horses, their hooves hitting the ground as they thundered along. They were making the tracks she had been hoping to find. She could smell the sweat that streamed from their manes.

Horses. Horses meant man, and man meant food. Lola kept quiet, though, because man also meant guns. Wild dogs knew better than to get close to men with guns but she did not want to alert the pack just yet.

There! A single hoof print caught Lola's eye. She headed toward it, and ordered the other dogs to stay close behind.

"But the mountains are that way," Pepe barked.

Lola ignored Pepe and continued on, searching and sniffing. The horses had passed through this way; she could almost see their ghostly forms. Where were their tracks?

Suddenly Lola found what she had been looking for, the river of horse tracks, one U-shaped hoof on top of another, a sure sign that several horses had been running together.

The dogs all stopped and sniffed.

"Horses have passed through here since sunup," said Nini, his whiskers starting to quiver. A horse had once almost trampled Nini, who got caught underfoot in a village raid. The horse miraculously stepped only on his tail but the heavy hoof took off several inches so that Nini had the shortest tail of all the dogs. He never wanted to get that close to a horse again.

"The horse tracks will lead us to food," Lola said. "We will follow the horse tracks and we will eat."

"Or the horse tracks will lead us to man who will eat us instead," Joaquín sneered. Joaquín had been seething all morning, still angry that Lola had shared the mouse with Dolores and not with him. And still angry at old Chili, for if he had not died in the middle of the fight, Joaquín might have won his battle with Lola, and the dogs would now be his.

Lola shook her head. "We must follow the horse tracks to man and to food," she said as she hastened along.

The dogs followed. They had no choice. They followed the horse tracks, galloping along like horses themselves. Lola led the way, with her desert-colored fur, then Bombom, his white coat marked by a black eye patch, and Dolores, so stunning and unusual with her long red fur like that of a fox. Behind these three, the other dogs loped along, a mix of black, brown, white, and gray.

Lola held her head high and gazed straight ahead. She could not let the other dogs see her doubt. She worried that the horse tracks could lead nowhere, or that the horses could be a hundred miles away by now.

No, the electric-charged air kept her running along. The horses were not that far away. Lola could smell their earthy aroma all around.

Then she spotted something, off in the distance, jutting out of the desert, something big and amazing. A giant rock? It seemed to call to her and soon the other dogs noticed it too. They galloped in its direction.

"What is it?" Mela called.

"Is it Pancho Villa's cave?" barked Pedro. "If it is, I get the first bite of goat jerky!"

The dogs ran and ran toward the huge shape. Suddenly, Lola stopped short and the other dogs piled up behind her.

"*Hacienda*," said Dolores, panting hard, her eyes bleary.

"What?"

"We've come to a *hacienda*," Dolores continued, and she plopped down on the ground, exhausted.

The dogs gaped with wide eyes.

"My *abuelo* lived on a *hacienda*," said Nini in a hushed tone. "My mama told me he was a fancy dog before he ran away and joined the wild dogs. Is this the *hacienda* where my *abuelo* lived?"

"Of course not," scoffed Joaquín. "Your family came from Puebla."

The dogs stared at the tall stone facade that reached high into the sky. A few of the dogs had seen *hacienda*s in the past, but some had never seen one before. Still, they all knew that the *hacienda* was the biggest type of house in all of Mexico. The *hacienda* was even bigger than many villages. In fact, the *hacienda* was its own village, with a magnificent house, stables, a general store, and a school. The *hacienda* had horses and cattle and many workers, mostly Indians, and the *hacienda* always had a *patrón*, who was very rich and ruled his estate from a mighty horse. And the *patrón* always carried a gun.

The rich man on his mighty horse who always carried a gun was one reason the villagers and the Indians were willing to fight in the Revolution. They did not want this man to rule their lives forever.

"We'd better run to the mountains before Pancho Villa eats all his goat jerky himself," said Nini, gulping with fear.

"The *hacienda* will be filled with food," Lola said.

"But Pancho Villa has goat jerky," Nini said weakly.

"The journey into the mountains could take many days," Lola said. "Raiding the *hacienda* is our only chance for survival."

The dogs stared toward the stone fortress, which was surrounded by a high, heavy metal gate.

Lola began walking forward and the dogs fell in line single file behind her. They grew more quiet and nervous the closer they got. By now, the dogs were practically tiptoeing and holding their breaths as they nervously inched along.

Suddenly, the *hacienda* gates swung open and a horse charged out; the rider waved a pistol high in the air.

The dogs scattered, yelping at the sight of man and horse.

"The rock, the rock" barked Lola, and the dogs rushed behind a nearby rock, cowering at the sight of the man on the horse, wildly waving his pistol above his head and yelling as if angry at the gods, as if furious at the whole world.

"I'll shoot any revolutionaries who dare to come near my *hacienda*," he shouted.

The dogs crouched closer to the ground, hoping to make themselves even smaller than they already were. Nini actually climbed on top of Mela.

"God help you, Pancho Villa, if I ever see your ugly face, I will happily shoot you through the heart myself!" the man continued. "You've destroyed Chihuahua with your Revolution, destroyed our old ways of living with your nonsense about saving peons!"

The man dug his spurs into his gleaming black stallion and rode off, galloping through the desert and leaving behind a cloud of dust that made the dogs cough.

"Oh, this is terrible," cried Mela, as she climbed out from under Nini. "That man is so angry and scary. I don't like people. I don't like them at all. We must run away." She turned and began to run, taking Nini with her.

"Come back," Lola barked. "You'll be killed out there by yourselves."

The dogs made a sudden stop and turned around.

"Maybe we should forget about finding Pancho Villa," said Nini with woeful eyes. "If that man kills him, I don't want to be nearby when he does."

"This just proves that Pancho Villa needs our help more than ever," Lola said. "We've just got to find him now."

With that, salty dog tears began to well in Nini's eyes. "I'm not sure I want to find Pancho Villa. I just want his goat jerky."

"We will find Pancho Villa and he will share his goat jerky," Lola said firmly, "but for now, we need food and the *hacienda* is our only chance."

"Are you going to find us some sausages?" Joaquín said in a slow, mean voice. "Because the last sausages you found were so delicious."

Lola ignored Joaquín and pushed her chest against the pack of dogs still huddled against the rock; she pushed against them to show her strength.

"What's wrong with you all? Raiding a *hacienda* is just like raiding a village. What happened to your bravery?"

Just then the dogs heard a terrible commotion from within the tall thick wall that surrounded the *hacienda*, horses stamped and snorted, men yelled, and women hollered. Two gunshots rang out and the *hacienda* gate was flung open again. Once more the dogs cowered behind the rock, crouching even closer to the ground and burying their heads under their paws. Only Lola dared to peek.

Several men sat on uppity horses who chomped madly on their bits. Indian servants darted about, carrying sacks on their skinny shoulders and then tossing them into a huge pile in the center of the courtyard. Women ran back and forth shouting orders and yelling at children to get out from underfoot. A turkey scurried by. Lola watched the excitement with big eyes.

The men on horseback took off through the gate, following the dust trail of the first horseman. When they had gone, several Indians slammed the heavy gate shut.

"Oh, let's run away," Mela cried. "I don't like these men, I don't like them at all."

At that moment, Lola's nose went crazy, shooting up into the air and sniffing in every direction. "Pig roasting on a fire," she barked. "Pig entrails and pig hooves and pig ears. How I love to chew on a salty pig ear."

"I love a good pig ear myself," said Dolores, a happy smile crossing her exhausted face. "Do you really think we could find some pig ears?"

"Or pig snout," said Manny with a dreamy gaze.

"I'm sure those *muchachas* will gladly feed a pack of wild Chihuahuas some of their roasting pig," said Joaquín with a scowl. "We'll just trot in, gather round the fire, and say pretty please."

"Shut up, Joaquín," growled Bombom. "No one wants to listen to you. I am sure Lola has a plan."

With that, all the dogs turned toward Lola.

"Of course I do," she promptly answered. "I'm going in and you're going to wait here."

"Bring back a long line of sausages for all of us to share," Joaquín gloated.

Bombom barked. "But how will we know you're okay, Lola? What if you need help?"

"You'll come with me," Lola said. "And you can run back and warn the others, or call them in when I find the pig ears, because I will find the pig ears. I can smell them now."

"I'm going too?" Bombom gulped. "But I'm not as brave as you, Lola."

"Yes, you are," Lola said, poking at Bombom's face with her nose. "I need you to be my scout."

And so Lola, with Bombom by her side, ran off toward the *hacienda*, while the other dogs crouched behind the rock and hoped for the best, for plenty of pig ears and pig snouts for everyone.

SEVEN

The *hacienda* was enormous. It stretched far into the desert and included a main house, a chapel, a store, servants' quarters, horse stables, and cattle pens. It was in fact the most important *hacienda* in the entire state of Chihuahua as it was owned by the wealthy and powerful Terrazas family.

But all that Lola and Bombom could see was a towering black metal gate attached to a high adobe wall. The dogs stared at the mighty gate and wondered how they would ever pass through.

"It's impossible," Bombom whispered.

"Nothing is impossible," Lola replied as she began to pace back and forth. "There's got to be a way."

The two dogs searched for several more minutes for a way in but the adobe wall seemed impenetrable.

"We could just wait by the gate until someone opens it for the horses," Lola said.

"And get trampled to death? I don't think that's a good idea."

"Hey," someone yelled.

"Who said that?" Lola barked.

"Me, over here. Say, could you do an *hombre* a favor?"

The two dogs looked around but saw no one.

"Hey," someone yelled even louder. "Aren't you paying attention? I'm right here, by the bush." And then Lola spotted a prairie dog blinking at them from beneath a creosote bush that was growing beside the adobe wall. The black-tailed rodent was sitting upright on his hind legs and rubbing his tiny front paws together, all the while rapidly blinking his black beady eyes.

"What do you want?" Lola asked.

"I can't get under the wall—someone filled up my usual hole with dirt. But it wouldn't be hard for you to dig it out. It's right here." The prairie dog pointed to a spot near the wall, just beside the bush. "Dig it out for me, and then you can squeeze through too. I know they've been planning a *fiesta* for days . . . and there's lots of food in the kitchen," the prairie dog continued in a singsong voice.

Lola stared at the bossy prairie dog. For a split second, she thought about eating him, but she decided against it. Maybe the critter would be of better use leading them to the food in the kitchen. And right now, Lola would dig through solid rock to get to that food.

So, following the critter's orders, Lola and Bombom dug in the soft dirt and finally the hole was big enough for the prairie dog to slide through but it was still not big enough for the dogs.

"*Adiós*," the prairie dog called as he scurried away. "Don't give up! You wild dogs are awesome—you can do it."

Lola and Bombom continued to dig until their front paws became raw. Finally, Bombom pushed his way through to the other side. "I made it," he called, his mouth filled with dirt. Soon Lola pushed through as well.

Once on the other side, the dogs could not believe their luck in finding several clay pots clustered together and overflowing with blooming red and pink geraniums, giving Lola and Bombom an instant hiding place. But it was unlikely, considering the noise and commotion that engulfed the huge courtyard, that anyone would have noticed two Chihuahuas.

Lola and Bombom saw people hurrying across the courtyard carrying all sorts of things—chairs, tables, trunks and boxes.

A woman had an armful of fancy party dresses, a mishmash of lace, velvet, and silk, and she threw it on the ground beneath a tumble of deep pink bougainvillea. Another woman came up and threw a large assortment of shoes on top of the pile.

"Curse the revolutionaries who ransacked and burned *Quinta* Carolina, Señor Terrazas's summer house, when his daughter and her husband were staying there," the shoe woman cried.

"Both have disappeared and no one knows what's happened to them," the dress woman added. "No wonder the Señor has taken off to find Pancho Villa himself. He will capture and kill him."

"Pancho Villa must pay for destroying the *patrón's* favorite summer house and terrorizing his daughter," the shoe woman said.

"No one knows where Pancho Villa is, no one has seen him for weeks, and now the American president has sent troops to Mexico to find him." A man clutched at his black hair and wildly shook his head. "We've got to escape before the revolutionaries come, for they will burn this *hacienda* to the ground."

"Where will I go?" the woman wailed. "I've lived here at *Hacienda* San Diego my entire life."

Pancho Villa sure has made a lot of people mad, Lola thought. *No wonder he's hiding in the mountains.*

As the woman fell into the man's arms, Lola sensed her chance; she began running toward the house, hoping and praying that Bombom was smart enough to stay on her heels. He was. The dogs ran through the courtyard until they came to an open door that led into the main house. Passing into the house, they ran through dark, cool rooms, their nails clicking against gleaming black-tiled floors.

"Where are we going?" Bombom barked as they ran.

"We've got to find the kitchen," Lola answered. "I wish that prairie dog had told us where it was."

At that moment, the dogs heard a door open and so they scrambled under a nearby table. From their hiding place, they watched as heavy boots marched by. Lola's nose went crazy as the smell of pig hit her like a dust storm.

She crouched under the table, determined to bring pig meat back to her pack. After the sausage disaster she wouldn't let her dogs down again.

The same door swung open again, and a fat lady carrying a big black pot waddled in, bringing the warm aroma of red beans with her. The door continued swinging back and forth, and squeaking as if dying a terrible death. When it finally stopped, the fat woman returned, without the pot. She pushed through the door once more, again setting off the terrible squeaking. The third time the woman passed through, Lola dashed through the swinging door; she made it just before the door could catch her tail.

She found herself in the *hacienda*'s massive kitchen. Had Bombom made it too?

Lola stood at full alert, absorbing her surroundings. She'd never seen such a big kitchen—its tiled counters, the color of red peppers, were covered with stacks and stacks of pots and pans, plates and bowls. About ten pots seemed to be boiling at once on top of a big black stove.

I've died and gone to the stars! Lola thought.

Everywhere she looked, food was piled high—steaming platters of rice; bowls of papayas, mangos, and bananas; plates loaded with rolls and breads. And there, on a table, smack in the middle of the room, was the star attraction—a whole roast pig on a serving platter, with a red apple stuck in his mouth, and yes, two ears and a snout.

"Lola, I've never seen so much food," Bombom barked, his tail wagging.

Thank goodness Bombom had made it through the swinging door.

"We've got to get the other dogs," Lola said. "They can sneak in too and we can eat that pig like pigs!"

"But what about the fat lady?"

"Yeah, what about the fat lady," said a terrible, snarling, mimicking voice.

Lola felt hot, sticky breath against her back. She turned and looked straight into the nose of the biggest, blackest, meanest looking dog she had ever seen. His black eyes flashed as he growled and crouched, ready to pounce on Lola and eat her alive.

I'm really done for this time, Lola thought as she stared back in horror. *There's no way I could possibly escape from this kitchen. I don't have a chance.*

EIGHT

"Down, Maxi, down, you bad dog."

A little girl had appeared in the doorway and was frowning and pointing her chubby finger at the massive dog. He immediately fell to the floor and looked at her with pleading eyes. Lola gaped at the little girl; her brown hair was styled in perfect curls, and her blue velvet dress was too fancy for everyday wear. In one hand, she held a porcelain doll that was her exact replica, right down to the velvet ribbon that tied back its curls. The little girl knelt down and scooped up Lola before she could escape.

"What a pretty doggy!" she exclaimed. "I love this pretty doggy."

The little girl was smashing Lola against her chest, squeezing the dog too tightly around the ribs with her chubby, greedy hands. "You're my doggy," she said, rocking Lola back and forth as if she were a little baby, scratching Lola's face with her starched lace collar.

Lola tried in vain to bite the girl but she knocked her head with her knuckles.

Ouch!

Lola looked down, horrified to see Bombom cowering beneath a chair and the killer dog Maxi still obediently lying on the floor but glaring at Bombom with ferocious eyes that flashed one silent message: I'll kill you.

"Maxi, you be a good boy or Ramona will spank you," the girl said, before turning and running out of the kitchen through the swinging door. Her tiny feet tripping along the hallway, she ran fast, passing door after door in the gigantic, empty house, until she finally came to a long winding staircase.

Ramona stood at the bottom and looked up. Lola, gasping for air through the girl's tight grasp, looked up too, her heart sinking faster than a stone in a lake.

For all Lola knew, Maxi had already swallowed Bombom in one nasty gulp. Lola struggled against Ramona's scratchy collar, growling and bearing her teeth. She had to save Bombom, she had to. It was her fault that he had come along in the first place.

"Stop squirming," Ramona said meanly, rapping Lola's head with her knuckles again.

Lola snapped, almost taking off the girl's finger, which had wagged too close to her nose.

"Don't be bad," Ramona said, holding Lola out with straight arms and scowling, her dark eyes narrowing. She then switched to a high singsong voice, "Wait until you see where I'm taking you."

Clutching Lola more tightly than ever, Ramona began climbing the long staircase, setting down her laced black boots on each step in a deliberate manner. Each agonizing step took Lola further away from Bombom, the food, and her pack, which was still waiting in the desert. Again Lola thrashed, kicking her legs, but the girl just squeezed harder until Lola could barely breathe.

Ramona finally reached the top step. She walked along another corridor, again passing door after door. At the end of the hallway, she reached the door she wanted. She pushed the carved wood door open and stepped into a room that shocked Lola.

The room was huge, big as ten village huts stuck together, and the ceiling was as high as the room was wide. It was furnished with elegant red-cushioned chairs, gold statues of angels on white plaster pedestals, and a variety of cabinets and trunks of carved wood. A vast stone fireplace with a thick marble mantle faced a four-poster bed with a gauzy white canopy. Above all the splendor hung a crystal chandelier, sparkling like a thousand stars.

Ramona pushed the door shut and turned the key in the lock. She walked to an oversized window and looked down into the terrible chaos that was still going on in the courtyard. Her grip began to loosen and Lola could finally turn away from Ramona's scratchy collar to see that the courtyard was swarming with men and women running around like chickens with no heads. Several carriages stood about and some men were shoving children and women inside the carriages while others threw bags on top. The jumpy, spooked horses could barely stand still.

"Poor little doggy," Ramona said, petting Lola's back. "All alone in the world. No Mami. No Papi. How sad for the little dog not to have Mami or Papi anymore." The little girl began petting Lola with a heavy hand, almost slapping her as she went into a strange trance.

Lola's head spun until she saw stars. Here she was held hostage by a peculiar little girl, upstairs in a fancy bedroom with the door locked, her pack waiting out in the desert for her and Bombom to return with food. And poor Bombom, perhaps already eaten by the killer dog Maxi.

Raiding the *hacienda* was the biggest mistake Lola had ever made. She wondered why it had ever seemed like a good idea.

Oh, Padre, how do I get out of this terrible mess? Lola knew Cuauhtémoc would never, ever let a child capture him.

Ramona began walking around the room, clutching Lola as she regarded the finery that filled every corner. The open door of a wood cabinet revealed a row of long fancy dresses bedazzled with satin ribbons, pearls, and embroidery. A dressing table was laden with beautiful silver hairbrushes and ornate hair combs.

In all the villages that Lola had raided, she had never come across so much finery. She knew the village women had one dress each, not one hundred. There was so much more—a collection of guitars, a row of polished black boots, a shelf of feathered hats. The more Ramona looked, the sadder she became until tears streamed down her cheeks. Even her brown curls seemed to coil more tightly with pain.

"Oh, Papi, you'll never get to play your guitar again. Remember how Mami would dance through the room as you sang?"

Ramona came to an oil painting hanging against the wall; it showed a man and woman so handsome their beauty seemed to radiate out from the painting and cast a glow around it. The couple held dramatic poses: the woman clutched a fan against her bosom, the man displayed a gold dagger above his head. As Ramona stared, she began to suck on her thumb. She sucked and sucked and Lola grew worried that she might spend the rest of her life trapped in the arms of this thumb-sucking girl. And then, like catching the scent of mice in the wind, Lola caught in her own heart the sadness swimming through Ramona's—it was the same sadness Lola felt about losing Cuauhtémoc. She understood that Ramona deeply loved the people in the painting.

The sound of several gunshots and neighing horses snapped Lola back to the trouble at hand. *I have to escape.*

And then, she heard a rustling noise. They were not alone.

Ramona instantly perked up. Turning away from the painting, she wiped her tears and began to giggle.

"Oh, my babies. I almost forgot my babies." Ramona carried Lola to the four-poster bed and pulled back the gauzy canopy to reveal a sleeping heaven of plump white pillows floating like clouds upon a pile of silky sky-blue sheets.

"Wake up, little girls," Ramona called. "I have a new sister for you."

A rustling from beneath the covers set Lola on edge. *Now what?*

"Don't be lazy," Ramona continued. "You've got a new sister, just like I promised. You've always wanted a sister."

The rustling continued and suddenly two heads poked out from beneath the covers. Two tiny Chihuahuas, the smallest Lola had ever seen, peeked out, trying to focus their sleepy eyes. Both dogs had white coats with brown spots and long pointy ears. The dogs looked identical, like twins.

Ramona began to pet these dainty dogs, who with their sleek coats and perfectly groomed nails were clearly as spoiled as Ramona, as spoiled as whoever lived in this fancy room. Pink silk ribbons dangled from their necks and they appeared to be wearing some kind of clothing that Lola could not yet make out.

"*Mamacita*, I wasn't done resting and she woke me," the slightly smaller dog complained. Lola thought this one was the funnier looking one, with its round bulging eyes that were much too big for its tiny rat's face.

"I'm sorry, *mi amor*. It's been so difficult to sleep with the terrible noise," said the other, as small as a baby rat herself, but slightly more pleasant to look at. "And lunch is late today. We've usually eaten by now!"

Lola knew Ramona could not hear a word the dogs said as they continued on about the noise, the difficulty in sleeping, and the forgotten lunch. On and on they whined, one complaint piled upon another like a big pile of dung in the cattle pen.

If the dogs ever stopped complaining they might spot Lola, who was now sitting on the bed almost directly before them. The moment had to come and finally . . .

"Ewww, *Mamacita*—a wild dog! Help, help, a wild dog!"

"Quiet down," Ramona said, for all she knew was that her dog was barking as if confronted by a coyote.

A sickening feeling overwhelmed Lola as she realized just what these dogs were. "Foot-warmers"—the lowest of the low as far as Lola was concerned. She'd heard about a relative who had gone off to become a foot-warmer in a *hacienda*. The dog's sole purpose in life was to warm the feet of its wealthy owners on cold nights. The dog never ran outside or hunted mice; it never chased lizards or slept in the warm sun. It stayed indoors all day so as not to become dirty, and every night it slept at the bottom of the humans' bed upon their feet.

Even worse, Lola realized, these dogs were wearing dresses! And what dresses! The *perrillos'* little dresses were decorated with the Mexican flag, a flounce of red, white, and green stripes with the famous coat of arms—an eagle holding a snake in its beak perched on top of a prickly pear cactus. Lola had seen the Mexican flag once, hanging from a pole in a village, and her *padre* had told her what the picture meant.

Lola glared at the little dogs and had an overwhelming urge to show them who she was, not some random dirty wild dog, but Lola, leader of the pack of wild Chihuahuas in the great state of Chihuahua. She stood tall, puffed her chest and growled.

"Oh, *Mamacita*, that wild dog's crazy," the small one yelped. "She's covered with dirt and it's making a mess on the bed. Who let her in the house?"

"Now, Clarita, we should show our manners, after all, we are the privileged dogs. Not every dog has our advantages."

The mother dog turned to Lola and said stiffly, "How do you do? I am Bambi, and this is my beautiful daughter, Clarita."

Before Lola could answer, the bedroom door began to rattle. It rattled and rattled as someone shook the doorknob from outside.

"Ramona, let me in," a woman cried through the door. "We've got to leave right this minute. The carriage is waiting out front to take us to Mexico City."

Ramona put her hands against her ears and began shaking her head wildly from side to side. "No, *Tía*, I want to stay here in case Mami and Papi come back."

"Ramonita, they're not coming back. We have to go now. Open the door!"

What happened next stayed in Lola's bones for the rest of her life.

She would never forget a heavy boot kicking against the door with a force she felt in her chest.

The door flying open and the hysterical woman running to the bed and grabbing little Ramona.

The woman, older than the beautiful lady in the painting, was shaking all over as if possessed by *El Diablo*.

Lola felt the woman's sharp words about danger coming at her like knives from all directions. The woman pulled Ramona to her chest and ran from the room in a flash; Ramona left anguished screams in her wake. A man had rushed in with the woman, appealing to the Blessed Virgin of Guadalupe for forgiveness before taking a small box from his pocket, pulling out a match, and swiping it against the rough side of the box.

Never could Lola erase from her mind the way he glared at the flame of the match with his red demon eyes.

"Pancho Villa, you'll take nothing from us because there'll be nothing left to take," he cried as he threw the match into the open closet. It landed beneath the row of beautiful dresses.

As the man turned to run from the room, a single thought gripped Lola's mind: *Don't shut the door!*

For if he slammed the door, the dogs would be trapped as the dresses burst into flames and the fire engulfed the room. Lola had on occasion imagined her own death, but it was never burning in a fire with a couple of spoiled, complaining foot-warmers wearing dresses decorated with the Mexican flag.

As the man ran out, his hand reached back to grab the doorknob. He began to slam the door shut, but then, a miracle—a gust of wind pushed the door back open.

Lola was amazed, but she knew what had happened.

Chili. Good old Chili. He had saved her life again. Lola jumped up and down on the bed with relief.

"*Mamacita*, what's happening? I want my lunch."

Lola whipped her head around to see Clarita pouting from under the sheets.

"Now, Clarita, I am sure someone will bring our lunch when it's ready," Bambi replied. "Patience is a sign of good manners."

Lola exploded. "There's no lunch! We've got to get out of here."

"Please don't use that tone with us," Bambi said firmly.

"Look, the dresses are burning, and it won't take long for the fire to jump to the bed."

"*Mamacita*, look—the closet's burning!" Clarita barked as if she had made this discovery herself. Indeed, by now the closet was ablaze, the dresses crackling and popping and shooting off sparks.

"Jump off the bed," Lola barked. "Run out the door."

"We've never jumped from the bed," Bambi barked back. "It's too far and we might injure a bone. We're both extremely delicate and unusually small due to good breeding."

Lola wondered why she was bothering to save these spoiled, ridiculous foot-warmers who would rather burn to a crisp than injure a bone. She peered over the bed. True, the stone floor was a far drop, but the fall could not hurt more than catching on fire.

Lola turned to the pile of fluffy white pillows. She clamped a corner of one in her teeth and tugged with all her might.

The dense pillow, stuffed with thousands of downy goose feathers, barely budged. Still, she tugged, determined, inching it off the bed until, thump, both she and the pillow fell to the floor, Lola first and the pillow on top.

"*Ay, caramba*," she muttered.

Lola climbed out from under the pillow and looked up at the little girls, staring down with worried faces. "Jump," she commanded.

Behind Bambi and Clarita angry orange flames were devouring the armoire, the beautiful dresses were now white ash swirling in the air and settling on their tiny apple heads like snow.

"Jump, Clarita," Bambi barked at her terrified daughter. Bambi nudged Clarita's bottom with her nose and she toppled off the bed, down onto the pillow, yelping the entire way.

At least Bambi has some sense, Lola thought, as Bambi jumped right beside Clarita.

"I lost a shoe; go get my shoe," Clarita whined, and indeed, she'd lost one of her little knitted red-and-green booties.

"Forget the shoe," Lola barked. "Follow me!"

The two tiny dogs stood and began to shuffle off the pillow but they kept tripping over their little dresses.

"I can't walk," Clarita cried, quickly losing her other three shoes. "I never walk. I'm always carried everywhere I go."

"No one's going to carry you now," Lola barked. "You've got to walk."

With quivering noses, the two pampered dogs followed Lola, tripping every other step. The dogs passed through the doorway and began their way down the long, empty hallway that seemed to stretch on forever. By now Clarita was openly bawling as she stumbled on the hem of her red, white, and green dress.

"Where are *Señor* and *Señora* Terrazas," she cried. "Why did *Tía* Elisa take little Ramonita out in such a rush? They wouldn't let me walk alone. Where's Yaya with our lunch? She's always on time with our rice and chicken. Where is everybody?"

Where was everybody indeed! The house was completely still, not a soul in sight, and not a sound, except for the crackle and pop of the fire spreading through the bedroom. Clarita suddenly stopped crying and became silent, as if the realization of her situation had finally knocked upon her thick little head.

"You've got to move faster," Lola barked. "We don't have all day!"

"But where are we going?" Bambi asked.

"I've got to find my *compadre* Bombom," Lola answered, her body shaking with a terrible dread. Bombom was dead. How could he have survived that evil dog? Still, she had to look for him, just in case. "We have to find the kitchen. Hurry! I know it's down this hallway and down the stairs."

They trotted along quickly, Lola and the tripping little girls, and finally they came to the wide staircase. Halfway down the stairs on the landing, she turned back to see Bambi and Clarita still standing at the top.

"Come on," Lola called, frantic. "The fire is getting angrier!"

"We can't," they both whined.

"We've never gone downstairs alone before," said Bambi. "We're not allowed unless *Señora* Terrazas takes us. We don't have permission."

"No one's here and the fire waits for no one," Lola yelped.

"We can't make it in our dresses," Bambi said. "These fine garments weren't meant for walking, especially not down the stairs. And besides, they're brand new. We got them for the *fiesta* and they'll be ruined."

Lola felt like she had fallen into a deep, deep hole. Why couldn't she just leave these silly dogs, an embarrassment to all dogs everywhere. Why did she feel responsible for them?

"Can I help?"

What! Who said that?

"Maxi!" the little girls shouted.

Lola turned quick as a flash, horrified to see the big black evil dog bounding up the stairs directly toward her, his pink tongue wagging from side to side.

"Stop," Lola growled, baring her teeth, hunkering down and ready to lunge. "What'd you do with Bombom. Stay back, or I'll attack!"

Lola would avenge Bombom's death; she would rip Maxi to shreds and make him pay for his savagery.

"I'm right here!"

What?

And there was Bombom, running up the stairs and standing beside Maxi, as if they were friends! Lola's heart soared but so did her alarm as she noticed a huge plume of smoke barreling down the hallway.

"We've got to get out of here! There's a fire upstairs."

"I'll get the little girls," Maxi barked, and he kneeled down beside Bambi and Clarita.

As if they had practiced a hundred times, the two Chihuahuas climbed onto Maxi's back, digging into his fur with their sharp little claws.

"Go, Maxi, go!" Clarita shouted in glee and together they bounded down the stairs.

With no time for questions, Lola licked Bombom's face and together they ran after Maxi and the little girls.

"Whee, faster," Clarita barked as Maxi galloped down the long hallway.

"The kitchen, go find food in the kitchen," Lola barked, running to catch up with Bombom by her side.

The five dogs headed toward the *hacienda* kitchen. But Lola stopped short and let the other run on without her when she came to the doorway that led to the *hacienda*'s main entrance; she had to make a detour, an extremely important detour. She had to find her pack and lead them to food.

NINE

Lola skulked into the courtyard, the same one she had passed through when she first snuck into the *hacienda* with Bombom. This courtyard, which had been the scene of such chaos earlier, was now completely deserted. The screaming people, the neighing horses, the wild children, the scurrying Indians, gone, gone, gone.

All that they had left behind was in the courtyard piled high as the Sierra Madre Mountains—the shoes and clothes, pots and pans, blankets and tablecloths, the suitcases and family paintings, the many wonderful things that they couldn't stuff into the carriages were left behind like rubbish.

Lola wondered why the *hacienda* folks had so many things, more than they could ever fit into their carriages, while the villagers had almost nothing at all, barely a shawl or shoes or even food. She ran across the courtyard and through the wide-open gate, out into the open desert where she gasped a huge breath of relief as the wind blew across her face.

How could those silly foot-warmers stand to be indoors all day, sitting in bed like porcelain dollies? Didn't they know the true joys of being a dog? Being stuck inside just wasn't natural. A dog was meant to run free.

The faster Lola ran the more eager she was to see her pack. Lola loved her pack, every single dog, well, except for Joaquín, who had been acting more hateful with every passing day.

Lola spied a rock in the distance, the rock where she had told the pack to wait for her.

Then, a terrible, sickening feeling overcame her. What if the pack wasn't there? What if a coyote had caught them off guard, or what if Joaquín had convinced the pack to follow him? Why wouldn't Joaquín take advantage of Lola's absence to persuade the other dogs to follow him once again? What if they had been scared by the *hacienda* ruckus, the departing caravan of carriages.

By now too many what-ifs filled Lola's head, and she ran on even faster to see just what lay behind the rock.

Lola slowed to a walk as she approached the rock, expecting the worst as she cautiously crept around its side, that she would find no more pack, all the dogs would be gone.

But instead the most surprising sight greeted Lola—all the dogs were lying close together and gazing with rapt attention at Dolores, who was sitting before them and speaking in a quiet but commanding tone. So focused were the dogs on Dolores, they did not even notice that Lola had returned.

"Of course it's well known that Chihuahuas were once the royal dogs that lived in the Aztec temples," Dolores was saying, looking over the dogs with serene confidence. "They were called Techichi then, but they were the same breed essentially. If anyone has doubts about our history, you must take my word."

When Lola and Bombom had turned from the pack and headed toward the *hacienda*, Dolores knew she would have to take action to keep a desperate situation from turning even worse. As the other dogs squabbled about who would sit in the sliver of shade beside the rock, Dolores walked away from the pack to a quiet spot where she could talk with Chili alone.

"Dear Chili, look how far we have fallen," Dolores told the hovering spirit of Chili as she looked back toward the starving, thirsty, tired dogs, panting in the sand. "These dogs do not really understand the greatness of the Chihuahua. We are lost souls, wandering through the desert to find a man who we don't even know is alive."

Dolores hung her head and closed her eyes. "I think I'm ready to leave the world of dogs and man as you did, Chili. My old, aching body can't take much more."

Chili's answer came into Dolores's head as a whisper:

It isn't yet your time, Dolores. You promised Cuauhtémoc you'd watch over Lola and help her claim her power as a leader. You promised in the last moments of his life on that terrible day. But perhaps, Dolores, you have an even greater job. You need to help all the dogs.

Dolores lifted her head and pricked up her ears; she was so relieved that Chili was indeed still watching over her and the other dogs and sharing his wisdom.

"I know, these poor Chihuahuas have forgotten who they are," Dolores replied, gazing into the sky where she thought he might be hovering. "I look into their eyes and I see deep savagery. I don't see the dignity that once marked the Chihuahuas when we lived in the royal temples of the Aztec emperors. We knew our birthright. Our lineage was strong. My mother was the storyteller who spread this knowledge before me, and her mother before her, and so on for generations, one dog to the next. She whispered the stories to me when I was just a pup. She said, 'Dolores, you know the truth about the Chihuahuas. You know we are special, even though some have fallen from grace. You must hold this truth and share it. Do not let the stories die.'"

"It's true," Chili whispered. "You can't let these stories die."

"Hey, you old demented dog," Joaquín barked to Dolores from beside the rock, where he stood glaring. "Why are you out there talking to yourself?" He turned to the dogs.

"Can you believe Lola went to the *hacienda* and just left us here in the heat," he said, his tone heavy with exaggerated disbelief. "We'll surely roast. I say we run away now. This plan to find Pancho Villa is *muy estúpido*. Come, follow me back to the watering hole where we can drink the cool water and hunt for more iguana. Wasn't that iguana meat delicious?"

The iguana meat wasn't delicious. It had been tough, dry, and scaly, painful to swallow. Still, the idea gave the dogs something to ponder.

"Maybe the iguana meat wasn't so bad," Nini said.

"I could sure use a long, cool, stinkin' drink," Pedro added.

"Iguana meat washed down with a cool drink of water sounds divine," said Mela with a dreamy look.

"Lola and Bombom will return soon from the *hacienda*, and she will surely have food," Dolores said.

"Another long line of sausages?" Joaquín barked, a crazy, angry bark that made the restless, starving, miserable dogs cower.

"I want a sausage," Mela yelped.

"And soon you shall have it, my dear. Let me tell a story to help pass the time," Dolores said.

The dogs huddled together, tails between their legs, in front of Dolores.

"Once upon a time, a strong and proud Chihuahua lived as the favorite dog to the glorious Aztec ruler Montezuma," Dolores said. "They lived together in a golden temple and he governed the beautiful Valley of Mexico. Do you remember what I told you about the Aztecs and their city?" she asked the dogs.

"Tell us again, Dolores," barked Mela, who always enjoyed Dolores's stories.

"Well, the Aztecs lived in Mexico a long time ago, and they built their capital city Tenochtitlan right in the exact spot where Mexico City is now. Tenochtitlan, the great city, was the center of the Aztec world, and the Aztecs were mighty and strong."

"The iguana meat was most delicious," Joaquín barked more loudly. "I can't wait to eat more. Follow me! Let's go now and eat like kings ourselves."

But something in Dolores's voice began to soothe the tired dogs, who really did not wish to do anything but lie in the slight shade of the rock. "You see, Montezuma II, the last of the Aztec rulers, had hundreds of dogs in his temple, but one was his favorite," Dolores said.

"Which dog?" Mela asked with wide eyes.

"The dog's name was Itzcuintli, and he was a Techichi, our forefather," Dolores said. "You see, the Aztec people adored the Techichi. They knew that the breed had mystical powers, which allowed them to see into the future.

"This dog was our relative?" Mela asked in disbelief.

"Yes," Dolores answered firmly. "Where do you think we came from?"

The dogs wanted to hear more about the dog Itzcuintli who was loved by Montezuma and lived in a golden temple.

As the dogs settled down, Dolores told them how Itzcuintli was always by Montezuma's side—when he met with his advisors, when he went into battle, and when he lay down to sleep.

"You see, Itzcuintli had a grand role in his future. When the time came for Montezuma to journey to the underworld, Itzcuintli would be his guide and help him navigate across the deep river."

Dolores then told them of Mictlan, the lowest layer of the underworld. Every Aztec soul descended to the underworld of Mictlan to find eternal rest.

First, though, they had to make a dangerous journey that took four years. The dead were given magical powers and the aid of the god Xolotl to make this journey beneath the earth, and a dog always accompanied them. A Techichi, the ancestor of the Chihuahua.

"A true Chihuahua knows the honor of taking a great adventure," Dolores said.

TEN

"But that's enough for now," Dolores said. "Look, Lola has returned."

The dogs turned their heads and there was Lola, standing behind the pack, tall and proud as if she were Itzcuintli herself.

"We've found food!" Lola was thrilled to be barking out the best news she could imagine giving at this moment. "There's plenty of meat: pork, chicken, beef, and turkey. I smelled it all. The *hacienda* is burning, but if we're fast, we can eat our fill before the fire travels downstairs and reaches the kitchen. Come on!"

Quick as lightning, Lola whipped around and ran back toward the *hacienda*, hoping that it would still be safe to enter the kitchen.

Nini, Mela, Pedro, Pepe, Manny, Joaquín, and Dolores took off following Lola as she sprinted across the desert.

The pack was startled by the news of the fire but they were intent on chasing one big word: FOOD. The pack hurried through the gate of the hacienda, across the empty courtyard, into the house, down the long dark hallway, and finally, into the grand kitchen.

All the way, "Pork! Chicken! Beef! Turkey!" boomed in their heads, and they were ready to run through shooting flames to get some.

The dogs blasted into the enormous kitchen and began barking and yelping as they skidded across the tile floor. With wide eyes, they took in the unbelievable feast, the many platters piled high with delicious, salty meats.

"Where's Chili, because I know we've died and gone to heaven," barked Pedro, turning in a circle and chasing his tail, not knowing what else to do. "I have been a good dog. I did go to heaven, even though my stinkin' mama said I wouldn't."

Round and round Pedro went, snapping at his tail in his delirium.

"If the humans kill us, if they come at us with their brooms and guns, at least I'll finally have a full belly," Mela said, so dizzy she almost fell to the ground.

"No one will harm you; the humans have all left," Lola said. "But you must eat quickly. The *hacienda* is burning!"

Indeed, the kitchen was becoming hazy with smoke.

"Wait, who are those strange dogs with Bombom?" Joaquín asked.

Strange dogs? The room instantly grew quiet as the pack went into high alert. In unison, the dogs spotted Maxi, Bambi, and Clarita. Indeed, Bambi, Clarita, and Bombom were standing on top of a table, already gobbling from a platter of chicken, while Maxi, standing on his hind legs, balanced against the table with his front paws.

They looked up. "It's not nice to stare," Bambi said hotly before returning to her meal.

"*Mamacita*, wild dogs are everywhere," Clarita said with a huge dose of disdain, her little face scrunched tight.

"You looking for a fight," Joaquín said, baring his teeth.

"Forget about it," Lola barked. "Just eat! We don't have time for fighting."

The dogs did not need another invitation. They jumped onto chairs and from the chairs onto tables, and they began wolfing down the unbelievable, inconceivable mounds of tasty food. Enough it seemed to feed every single person in all of Mexico.

Is this why the villagers hardly ever had anything to eat, wondered Lola, *because the rich people kept all the food of Mexico hidden in this kitchen?*

Nini and Mela jumped onto a counter where they discovered a platter of *carne asada* already chopped for tacos.

"Yiyiyiyiyiyi," Nini barked, taking a huge mouthful, the spicy *carne asada* setting his tongue on fire. "Yayayaya" he barked as its oily, juicy goodness ran down his chin and whiskers.

For ten minutes, the kitchen was filled with the sounds of frenzied chomping, crunching, and gulping as the dogs ate and ate and ate. So intent were the dogs on inhaling the pork, chicken, beef, and turkey, they did not even hear the fire crackling and popping as it raged through the house.

Her eyes smarting, Lola lifted her head from a nearly clean platter of pork. Smoke was pouring into the kitchen. She looked around—half the dogs were lying on the tiled floor, groaning.

"My belly aches," Mela whined.

"We have to go now," Lola barked nervously.

"But I can't even stand," Nini said. "I'm bursting."

"Get up," Lola barked. "The fire's here." She ran around the kitchen in search of the dogs but she could hardly see through the heavy, black smoke. "Where's Dolores? Where's Bombom?"

"I'm here, Lola, but I can't walk. The smoke is too much for my old lungs," said Dolores, who lay on the floor under a table. "Just as Mela said, at least I'll leave this earth with a full belly. It was worth it! I've never eaten so well. The *lengua* was delicious, cooked to perfection with *jalapeños*."

"No, Dolores. You must run with us. You can make it."

But Dolores continued to lie listlessly on her side.

"Don't worry, Lola, I'll carry her," said Maxi.

"On your back? She couldn't hold on. She can't even stand."

"I'll carry Dolores in my mouth," Maxi said, standing over Dolores with a calm and confident look. "But first, help wrap this string of sausages around my neck. We may be full now, but we'll be glad for this food later."

Maxi had dragged a long row of pork sausages, twice as long as the string that Lola had stolen from the village just a day ago.

"Hang down your head, and I'll wrap them around your neck," said Bombom. The crafty dog snatched the first plump sausage and circled the string round and round Maxi's neck, until it draped like a beautiful golden necklace, the most beautiful and precious necklace in the world.

The dogs stumbled out of the kitchen into the hallway, which was so filled with smoke they could not see a thing. Smoke filled their eyes and ears; the hot floor scorched their paws. The pack ran through the hallway guided only by Lola, in the lead barking, "Straight ahead, keep going, almost there." By now flames were racing through the house. Here they came, dancing down the hallway, en route to the kitchen. The dogs ran past the flames, just in time, out into the fresh air of the courtyard and . . .

"Yiiiiyiiiiyiiii!" A terrible howling rose from someone in the pack. "My tail's on fire! My tail, my tail!"

"What . . . who . . ." Lola looked around wildly. In the courtyard she could see poor Manny hopping up and down like a jumping bean, his furry tail burning as bright as a glorious sunset.

The dogs started barking all sorts of crazy messages:

"It's the stinkin' *El Diablo*, angry that we ate his stinkin' food," yelled Pedro.

"Run, Manny, run away from the fire," shouted Pepe.

"The fountain, Manny, jump in the fountain!" barked Maxi, who had dropped Dolores from his mouth to get out the hasty words, the only ones that made any sense.

Luckily, Manny heard Maxi. He jumped into the stone fountain that stood in the center of the courtyard, and in a second his blazing tail was extinguished. There he stood, smack-dab in the middle of the fountain, as all the other dogs gathered around and quickly drank before dashing off.

With Lola in the lead, the dogs ran out of the courtyard, through the gate, and back out into the open desert. Maxi was right behind Lola—Dolores hung from his mouth by her scruff, Clarita and Bambi rode on his back, and the long row of sausages were wrapped around his neck. Next came Bombom, Mela, Nini, Pedro, Pepe, the soaking-wet Manny with his charred tail, and finally, Joaquín. The dogs ran until they reached the rock outpost from where they had started.

They collapsed into a heap, panting, coughing, whining, and still groaning from too much food. Here they lay, watching the *hacienda* as it exploded in flames; the enormous fire now hungrily consumed the entire house and all its remaining furniture, clothes, and paintings and food! The fire lit up the sky in orange and red, and it sent plumes of smoke straight up like long, black snakes.

Whatever was left of the house was now smoldering, igniting, melting, and torching. Embers were flying everywhere. The fire's heat was radiating in the already hot afternoon, and the dogs watched in wonder with panting tongues.

Lola suddenly became aware of someone weeping. She turned to see Clarita, her too-long tongue flickering in and out of her mouth like a lizard's as she caught tears streaming from her eyes.

"My dress is soiled and my life is destroyed," Clarita sobbed, giving up on trying to catch the tears. "Where's Ramona? Where is *Señora* Terrazas and *Tía* Elisa? Why didn't they take us with them? What are we supposed to do?"

As Bambi licked her face, the other dogs gathered around Clarita. As different as these spoiled dogs were from the pack dogs, something connected them. Somewhere deep inside Bambi and Clarita were still just dogs.

"Perhaps if we wait, *Señor* Terrazas will return," Maxi said, looking doubtful and scared, his black brows and black nose twitching. He had gently released Dolores from his mouth, and she lay before him with concerned eyes.

"Perhaps he will," Dolores said, not knowing who *Señor* Terrazas was, and why he left, but wanting to comfort Maxi who had saved her life.

Lola shook her head. "I'm sorry, Maxi, but *Señor* Terrazas is long gone." A funny feeling overwhelmed her. Why did Maxi care so much where that human went, and why did he want him to return?

"I'm sure he'll come back," Maxi said, sitting up straighter, his long nose pointing toward the scorching *hacienda*. "I'll wait here with Bambi and Clarita until he does."

Lola shook her head. "You can't stay here by yourself with these two little dogs. You'll be hunted by coyotes in no time."

"I've fought a coyote before," Maxi said with steely defiance, lifting his long nose even higher. He placed his big black furry front paws together. "Once when I was hunting with *Señor* Terrazas, I scouted a coyote and the *Señor* shot him dead."

"Come with us to find Pancho Villa," said Lola, not wanting to point out again that *Señor* Terrazas would not be around to shoot the coyote next time.

The mention of Pancho Villa's name sent Bambi and Clarita into a terrible tizzy. It was as if Lola had asked them to come with her to find the murderous lout, monster, and savage *El Diablo*. Bambi's eyes bulged from her head and Clarita's tongue began darting in and out of her mouth again, as if in spasms.

"Pancho Villa, no, no, no, that terrible man is the cause of all Mexico's troubles," Bambi barked in near hysterics. "He deserves to be shot by a firing squad."

ELEVEN

Standing under the beating sun with the *hacienda* burning in the distance, Lola bristled, feeling her own insides on fire.

"Pancho Villa is a Mexican hero," she said, stepping in closer to Bambi.

"Pancho Villa is a disgrace! An outlaw and a bandit," Bambi retorted, inching closer to Lola's nose.

"Hero."

"Bandit."

"Hero!"

"Bandit!"

By now the two dogs were glaring at each other. Bambi puffed out her chest and inched even closer so that Lola was looking right up her mini turned-up nose. Lola had never met a Chihuahua with such a stuck-up, turned-up nose.

All the Chihuahuas circled in more closely, waiting to see just how Lola would punish this disrespectful little dog who didn't seem to care one whit that Lola was the leader of the pack.

"Push her to the ground," said Nini.

"Show her you're the boss," added Manny.

As Bambi puffed up her chest and pushed out her nose, Lola quickly considered her options. She could easily jump on this spoiled brat and throw her to the ground—Bambi was half her size, even smaller—but Lola knew Maxi would jump in to protect his little friend. She liked Maxi and did not want to make him mad.

"We heard that Pancho Villa turns into a black coyote at night and runs with a pack that steals sleeping human babies from villages," Bambi said in a taunting voice.

"Who told you such a thing," said Lola, shuddering. Black coyotes were sorcerers with magical powers that were not always used for good.

"Why, *Señor* Terrazas, of course." Bambi looked to Clarita. "Don't you remember *Señor* Terrazas saying that babies throughout Mexico weren't safe with Pancho Villa on the loose?"

"Oh, yes," Clarita agreed. "Why would *Señor* Terrazas lie about such a thing?"

"Well my *padre,* Cuauhtémoc, met Pancho Villa, and he said Pancho Villa was a good, strong leader." At the mention of Cuauhtémoc, Lola was filled with a rush of good feelings.

"What kind of a funny name is 'Cuauhtémoc,'" sneered Clarita, butting in and pushing her own nose between the two.

Lola tipped her head to one side. "You don't know the name of the Aztec ruler of Tenochtitlan," she said with genuine surprise.

"We don't bother our pretty heads with boring information," Bambi said. "We're fancy dogs! We don't need to."

Lola turned away from the spoiled brats. She looked over to Dolores who was sitting beneath the arm of a silvery agave.

Dolores shook her head sadly and sighed. Dolores had told the Chihuahuas the story of Cuauhtémoc many times. The original Cuauhtémoc had lived in the Aztec temple at Tenochtitlan and had been a great leader of the Aztecs as they battled against the Spanish *conquistador* Hernán Cortés. Nephew to Montezuma, in 1520 he became the eleventh and last Aztec emperor until his capture by the Spanish. Lola's father had been given the special name by his uncle, who said he recognized a true leader the day he was born. Brave canine Cuauhtémoc deserved to be named for such a courageous human ruler of the Aztec people.

The terrible memory of the day Cuauhtémoc died almost took over Lola's mind but she quickly blinked it away.

"What does such a funny word mean anyway?" Clarita asked. "Sounds like I need to spit."

"One Who Has Descended Like an Eagle,'" Lola said, still blinking.

"One *what* who has descended like an eagle," Clarita snorted. "What are you talking about?"

"Excuse me," Dolores said softly. "But you have a descending eagle on the flag on your dress. Don't you know the story of the eagle and the Aztecs?"

Bambi and Clarita stared at Dolores blankly.

"Tell the story, Dolores," Mela said. "I love this story."

"Yes, tell us," echoed Manny and Nini, and with that all the dogs sat down and looked expectantly at Dolores.

"Well then, I will," said Dolores as she looked over the dogs. "I will tell the story so that Bambi and Clarita can learn this important history."

"Don't do anything for our sake," sniffed Bambi, but Clarita moved toward Dolores and pricked up her ears.

Dolores began: "A long time ago, long before the Techichis lived among the Aztecs, the Aztecs were a nomadic tribe roaming through Mexico as they did not have a city of their own. They became tired of wandering and wanted to build a city, but they didn't know where. One day they received a message from Huitzilopochtli, their god of sun and war, who said he would guide them to a magical place to build their city. Who remembers how the Aztecs would know when they'd reached the magical place?"

"I do, me, me," barked Nini, jumping up and down. "They'd know when they saw an eagle, perched on a cactus, eating a snake."

"Yes, an eagle, perched on a cactus, eating a snake," the other dogs chorused.

Dolores continued: "For the next two hundred years, the Aztecs wandered in the Valley of Mexico, always on the lookout for an eagle, perched on a cactus, eating a snake."

"Eating a stinkin' snake," Pedro couldn't resist yelling out.

"One morning, an Aztec priest was standing on the swampy shore of Lake Texcoco," Dolores said. "He looked out across the lake. On one of the lake's many small islands, he saw an eagle on a cactus with a snake wiggling in his mouth."

The Aztecs had found their home at last. They named the island Tenochtitlan, Place of the Prickly Pear Cactus, and they built the glorious Aztec capital city in honor of Huitzilopochtli.

Clarita wagged her tail with enthusiasm. "That's Mexico City? Why, Mexico City has the fanciest restaurants and the best hotels. We've been to them all with *Señora* Terrazas. And to think it's all because of an eagle."

"Please, Clarita, I'm not sure if that story is really true. It may just be a fairy tale to calm the *campesinos*," sniffed Bambi.

Lola's mind flashed on Bambi and Clarita, nestled in expensive pillows, and the kitchen at the hacienda, with its never-ending stock of food.

"Pancho Villa is hiding, but we're going to find him," said Lola. "We're going to help him so that he comes out of his cave and helps Mexico become strong again."

"I'd like to find that Pancho Villa and give him a piece of my mind," Bambi said with blazing eyes, her dress flouncing as she trotted about the circle of dogs. "I'll show him who's a hero to Mexico. Ha!" She tossed her head and trotted even faster.

"Let's settle down," Maxi pleaded, upset that the dogs were not getting along.

But Bambi had much more to say. "If it weren't for Pancho Villa, our *hacienda* wouldn't have burned to the ground."

"What? How can you blame that on Pancho Villa?" Lola said. "That man threw fire into the closet! It's his fault. Pancho Villa wasn't anywhere in sight."

"Villa's the one who started all the fighting," Bambi said, fuming with indignation. "*Presidente* Carranza was doing a perfectly good job taking care of Mexico until Pancho Villa began to stir up the hornets' nest. Jealous, I suppose. That's what *Señor* and *Señora* Terrazas said. Villa didn't have his own *hacienda* and servants, so he ruined it for those who did. He is not even a Chihuahuan but a poor boy from Durango with not a spec of good breeding. *Señor* Terrazas said that Pancho Villa worked on a *hacienda* himself, as a boy he was just a common worker. His parents were poor and he never even learned to read or write."

Bambi and Clarita exchanged knowing looks.

"Well, I'm not so sure that going off to find Pancho Villa is the best idea myself," Joaquín said with a sneer. "But I am sure that Pancho Villa would love to hear your opinion of him."

Bambi's eyes widened. "I do have a mind to march to that cave and tell Pancho Villa what I think. Where is this cave?"

"Up there," said Bombom.

"Where?"

"At the top of the Sierra Madre Mountains—at least, that's what Crow told us."

"Well, then," Bambi said, tossing back her head. "*Señor* Villa had better watch out, because I'm going to march to the top of the mountain and speak my mind."

"You tell him," Clarita barked.

"He's been causing trouble for years now with his ridiculous Revolution and his silly ideas of fairness, making life difficult for *Señor* Terrazas, and making *Señora* Terrazas always so nervous and upset," Bambi continued. "Remember, Clarita, how she used to hug us to her bosom and weep for hours. How can anyone expect a proper lady such as *Señora* Terrazas to give up the things that make life enjoyable—the beautiful clothes and the parties, with all the fanciest and most important people in all of Chihuahua coming to dance until dawn. The prettiest women and the handsomest men arriving in fine carriages, with even the horses draped in jewels. Why, Governor Treviño was on his way to the *hacienda* for a *fiesta* when it burned down. That was his food you all enjoyed. And now, look, the *hacienda* is gone. Gone!"

"Mommy, are you sure you want to climb up that mountain," Clarita asked with worried eyes. "How are we ever going to reach the top? I can't possibly walk all that way."

"Maxi will carry us, of course."

"Why not, what else are we going to do?" Maxi said sadly. "Lola's right. We can't stay here alone. Not safe."

"Fine," Lola said. "We're going to continue our journey to find the great Pancho Villa. You're welcome to come along to meet him. And when you do, you'll understand his power and see that he's a great leader. You'll learn how wrong your people were. And you can't speak badly about him either. I won't have it."

"It's only my good breeding and perfect manners that will keep me from describing *Señor* Villa as colorfully as I could," Bambi said, stamping the ground with one of her itty-bitty paws.

So with Lola in the lead, Dolores on her right, Maxi on the left (Bambi and Clarita on his back), and the rest of the pack following close behind, the dogs continued on their quest. With three new dogs, the group continued through the desert toward the towering Sierra Madre Mountains to find Pancho Villa.

TWELVE

The dogs plodded along through the dust. Lola marched proudly in the lead with her black nose pointed straight ahead. She lifted her white paws high and strode forward with purpose. Still by her side was Dolores, her long red fur matted and stuck against her emaciated body, and behind Dolores came Maxi with the teeny-tiny Bambi and Clarita riding on his broad back, and the string of sausages dangling from his neck. The littlest dogs gawked, eyes darting about; except for carriage rides to Mexico City they had never spent much time outside the *hacienda*. The other dogs trailed behind, hot and tired with hanging heads and panting tongues.

Suddenly, Maxi starting barking crazily into the sky.

"Woof, woof! Back off you murderous thief! You'll have to fight me before you take these innocent dogs. Why don't you find some snake your own size and leave us alone. We've had a hard day and we're on our way to find Pancho Villa, so back off."

The black dog was thrusting himself high into the air as if wishing to bite the sun, sweat flying off his fur, the sausage necklace bouncing around his neck.

Suddenly the dogs saw the object of Maxi's wrath. A big hawk was diving right toward the little dogs, his sharp and pointy talons aiming for their heads.

Thrown off Maxi's back by his sudden jumping, Bambi lay in the dusty dirt and watched in shock as he barked at the sky. He jumped up and down as if on fire, snarling and growling.

"I hope that outburst served some purpose because you tore and soiled my dress," Bambi said, mustering a big scoop of indignation even though the fall had knocked the wind from her little chest.

"You could have warned us!" Clarita had also been thrown to the ground. "You scared me! And one of those sausages knocked me in the head! You could've killed me."

"That hawk was diving straight at us," Maxi exclaimed. "He wanted to eat you. I'm sorry if I ruined your dresses, but I had to stop him. And I'm sorry about the sausage." Maxi shook his neck so that the sausages fell to the ground.

By now Lola had run over. "Hawks usually leave us alone unless they're really desperate or we've let our guard down. The little girls must have tempted him with their fresh clean scent on the wind. Thank you, Maxi. You saved their lives."

"Who's going to fix my dress," Bambi said, looking more cross by the second. "I don't have any of my other clothes. *Señora* Terrazas never let me wear anything that was stained or ripped."

"What other clothes?" Mela asked, her eyes wide with wonder as she approached the group. "How many dresses did you have?"

"At least one fresh dress every day and sometimes two. But that doesn't include our nightclothes," Clarita said. "Look! My dress is soiled too—a huge stain right in front and a tear on the ruffle." Bambi and Clarita looked at each other and burst into tears. "We're hot and tired and our dresses are ruined," Clarita cried.

"Maxi wasn't being careful and he should have used his manners," Bambi added.

"Well, isn't that terrible," said Joaquín with a nasty smirk, clearly delighting in the drama. "Little *perros* in pretty dresses decorated with Mexican flags and now all dirty because that *estúpido* dog tried to save their lives. You should be mad. Furious." Joaquín grinned from ear to ear and shook his head.

"Let's look at the bright side," Mela said, coming upon Clarita with a real look of concern. "Maxi saved your life. How lucky you are to have such a devoted friend, willing to risk his own life to save yours."

The little dogs looked unsure.

"We'll eat the sausages now; that'll make us feel better," Lola said. "Bambi and Clarita can eat first."

"I'm not sure I can eat under this kind of stress," Clarita said, jutting out her little chin and looking at all the dogs.

"I'll eat your stinkin' sausage," Pedro said, sniffing the dusty meat.

"Maybe we should rest for the night," Lola said, sensing the dogs' moods were about to collapse. "You all share the sausages and I'll find a safe spot to sleep."

So while the dogs ate, Lola paced about the desert until she found an outcrop of rocks that could shield the dogs. Lola poked around under the rocks to make sure a snake or scorpion wasn't taking a nap. Lola's black whiskers twitched and she shuddered. A snake would be the worst; she knew the swift damage a snake could bring. Once Lola was sure it was safe, she motioned the dogs in with her nose and, their bellies full, they crawled one by one into the cool hidden space.

Protected by the pile of rocks, the dogs relaxed. They were exhausted by the long day's many calamities, from the fire to the hawk. Bambi and Clarita began describing in great detail the many dresses that they had left behind, the embroidered smocks and knit ponchos, the silk gowns for evening affairs. With lively expressions, they discussed the colors and the patterns, the lengths of the sashes. They bickered about whether a collar was silk or satin, whether a button was made from pearl or stone.

The other dogs stared, mesmerized by this strange idea that a dog would wear a dress, and then that she would have not one but a dozen.

THIRTEEN

That night while her pack soundly slept, Lola crawled out from under the outcropping and sat beside Maxi, who was stationed outside keeping watch. Maxi refused to join the dogs in sleep and wouldn't let any of the other dogs take his place, even for a minute. Lola marveled that the big dog could survive on a few moments of dozing here and there.

The night was dark and quiet, with no moon, no breeze, and a cloud cover shielding the stars. Lola sat beside Maxi and stared into the surrounding blackness. Together they listened as a single coyote howled, calling his pack together with a high quavering cry and short yips. Another howl answered and then another until chorus of coyotes sang together.

Then came the barks, the cacophony of barks as the coyotes found one another in the night. Lola's fur bristled but she knew the coyotes were far enough away; they would not find the dogs.

With luck, that is, there were never any guarantees.

All the while, something weighed heavy on Lola's mind, something she couldn't understand and something she had to ask Maxi. Finally, when the coyotes had moved away and quiet returned, she found her voice.

"Why did you want that man to come back?"

"Which man?

"The man you lived with."

"You mean my master?"

A knot of disgust filled Lola's throat. "Why do you call that man such names, as if he's in charge of you?"

"He was in charge of me."

Lola couldn't believe such words even existed. "How can a man be in charge of a dog? A dog is in charge of a dog."

Maxi stared blankly into the pure black night. "I would come when he called," he said quietly, as if speaking to himself. "I would sit at his feet every evening as he smoked his pipe, and he would rub my belly with his slippered feet. When he had strong words with his wife, we would sit together outside in the late night. He would even hug my neck and say I was his only real friend in the world. I followed him anywhere. That brought me the greatest happiness of my life, serving my master."

"Serving a master brought greater happiness than running with your pack? Than this moment here, sitting in the night together, dog-to-dog? How can a person be so important? Most people I've come across wanted to smack me with their brooms."

Maxi looked at Lola and shook his head, his kind eyes glistening with wetness. "*Señor* Terrazas came to my village and took me from my mother and two brothers when I was just six weeks old. For many seasons, I loved and obeyed my master. It's true that I sometimes felt trapped living in the *hacienda*. Everyone expected me to be a mean guard dog. *Señor* Terrazas demanded that I show my teeth and act tough whenever anyone came to visit, but that's not really me. I hate growling at people; I'd rather lick their faces. But he was still my master and I obeyed his every word. But what about you and your quest to find Pancho Villa? Don't you want him to become your master?"

Lola shook her head. No, finding Pancho Villa was different. This quest was about helping this great leader, restoring Mexico's strength, and helping her pack become strong again too. It was about feeling Pancho Villa's power as her *padre* had so that Lola could be as good a leader as Cuauhtémoc had been. She would never want Pancho Villa to be her master. Lola, however, didn't want to hurt Maxi's feelings since he so clearly loved his master, so she kept quiet.

"Well, anyway, I don't believe that Pancho Villa is a black coyote who steals babies at night," said Maxi. "Bambi and Clarita were completely devoted to *Señora* Terrazas and she certainly hated Pancho Villa with a vengeance."

As the two dogs sat together, Lola remembered the many stories that Dolores had told of the Chihuahuas long ago, living in the Aztec temples with the Aztec rulers and priests.

If Dolores was telling the truth, then the Chihuahuas had lived with man, had served man, and had perhaps even loved man, just as Maxi had so clearly loved his master.

The idea of dog living so closely with man made Lola's head spin so fast that she sprung from her spot beside Maxi and ran out into the desert, into the wide-open freedom that was all she knew. She ran and ran as if to escape the idea of man and dog. The horror of Bambi and Clarita letting man dress them in little dresses nipped at her heels and sent her running even faster. Lola would never become the property of man. She was a free dog, and even Pancho Villa, when she found him, would never be the master of Lola.

No one would ever be the master of Lola. No one.

Lola stopped running and stared up into the sky. The cloud cover was starting to break apart and glittering stars began peeking through. One, two, three stars, then ten, then twenty stars sparkled above. Lola pricked up her ears; the desert bubbled with night activity, and she sensed the millions of insects, reptiles, and animals crawling, slithering, and running all around her.

The laughing, weeping, birthing, dancing, loving, and fighting all around filled the desert with an electric energy that sent a charge through Lola. A gentle wind blew across Lola's ears and in its rustle Dolores's words came back into her mind:

"Chili and I knew when Lola was young that she held the power to save the dogs. It's your obligation to turn around and follow Lola. Chili can't cross over until we do the right thing."

That is what Dolores had told the dogs and Dolores always knew the truth and she never wavered in her beliefs.

What if we could help Pancho Villa? Wouldn't we be helping Mexico's villagers and helping the Chihuahuas too?

This was the idea that started this journey, and the more Lola thought about this, the more the clouds cleared, and the more stars popped into the sky. In mere moments, the sky had turned from dark, cloudy, and empty to a sea of diamonds. Lola knew that every star held the soul of a dog, and she realized they were appearing to keep her company and to offer guidance on this journey.

Lola wished she could find Cuauhtémoc's star. She looked every night and not once had she recognized the star that she was sure belonged to her *padre*. She knew the stars that belonged to her *madre*, and to her *abuela* and *abuelo,* twinkled above too. She knew that since time began all the dogs that had lived in Mexico and had run through the desert and over the mountains had finally made their way to the sky.

Oh, Cuauhtémoc, which star are you?

Lola searched the vast sky. She had been looking for this one star all year, since her father had so suddenly left her all alone. Not finding his star made her feel so lonely.

Lola thought of her pack and the little dogs huddled under the rocks and wondered if they really could make it up the mountain to find Pancho Villa's cave.

Lola's heart was heavy with one sure realization: Dolores probably would not survive such a daring trek along the steep paths that offered no protection from the sun and wind, from snakes and hawks. Dolores was already struggling just to cross the flat desert floor.

"It's okay, Lola, you mustn't worry about me."

Lola jumped. *What*?! *Who said that*? *Was the wind playing tricks*?

Lola turned around and there was Dolores. She seemed to shimmer in the night. Lola felt as though all the Doloreses she had ever known were there with her. Lola saw the young beautiful Dolores that she had adored as a puppy, the Dolores who had licked her face that terrible night when her own mother disappeared. Lola certainly saw the strong and loving Dolores who had rushed in to comfort her on that terrible day last year when Cuauhtémoc was taken. But Lola also saw the feeble and failing Dolores, her beautiful fire-red fur now thinning and streaked with gray, her head straining to hold still against the shaking that often overwhelmed her weak muscles.

"Dolores, climbing the mountain will be challenging, even for the young dogs," Lola said.

"I know, Lola. I'm not sure I'll ever meet Pancho Villa but I'm certain the pack will. You must never doubt that this journey is your destiny."

"How can you be sure?"

"Just look at the sky."

Lola looked into the sky and a million stars now sparkled and glittered, replacing the black sky almost completely. A shooting star streaked across the sky. Another one followed faster than the first, and then another, and suddenly the sky blazed with a hundred shooting stars. Lola had never, ever seen such an amazing shower of light. At the same time, a mighty wind came up from the stillness. It whipped through the ocotillo cactus and blew in a flurry of tumbleweeds. The desert roared with this wind.

"What's going on, Dolores?"

"The ancient dogs are sending you a message, as is Chili. Lola, they are taking this journey with you. Don't be afraid. You are going up the mountain not just for Pancho Villa and the people of Mexico, and not just for yourself or the pack. Your journey is for all the future generations of Chihuahuas to come. Something important will be gained, Lola. Chili knows this too. He sent me a message in a dream. That's why I'm here now, to tell you that Pancho Villa is indeed sitting in a cave waiting for us, just as Crow said. I saw him sitting all alone on a rock in a dark, dark, place. He may not know what he is waiting for, but he's waiting for you, nonetheless. Don't fail him by not believing."

FOURTEEN

The next morning the dogs rose early, just as the sun began to lighten the sky. They crawled out from under their shelter of rocks and quietly continued their walk toward the Sierra Madre Mountains, through the mesquite, agave, and ocotillo.

Lola led the pack, with Bombom and Dolores beside her. Bambi and Clarita climbed back on to Maxi's back without saying a word about their disastrous fall the day before. Mela and Nini fell in line behind Maxi, and Pedro, Pepe, and Manny followed. Joaquín straggled at the rear, far enough behind so that he did not have to listen to the dogs' chatter, but close enough to feel security in numbers.

"If I wore a dress, I would want it to be green with shiny buttons," Mela said wistfully, her head swimming with the colors and patterns that Bambi and Clarita had described the night before. "Green would look lovely against my pure white coat."

"Dogs don't wear dresses," Nini remarked.

"Bambi and Clarita do," Mela said. "And who's to say other dogs couldn't wear dresses too? Maybe someday a human will give me a dress."

"I'm not sure those foot-warmers are really dogs." Joaquín could not resist throwing out insults.

"We heard that," Bambi shot back, "You're just jealous that we lived in a beautiful *hacienda*."

"Well, you certainly don't live in a *hacienda* anymore, do you?" Joaquín said. "Guess you're stuck with us mongrels."

Bambi stuck her nose in the air and turned around, letting the matter drop. The truth was the dogs were weary and the Sierra Madres loomed so large before them. How would they ever find the strength to climb to the top to find Pancho Villa's cave?

"What if we get to the top and Pancho Villa is gone?" asked Nini, voicing the fear many of the dogs shared.

"He won't be gone," said Dolores.

"How do you know?" said Manny.

"Yeah, how do you know?" echoed Pepe. "What if we climb all that way and the cave is empty? Or what if Pancho Villa chases us away, like so many humans have?"

"He might shoot us with his gun and cook us over his stinkin' fire," added Pedro with alarm. "We don't know! Some humans eat Chihuahuas."

Lola stopped walking and turned around to face her pack. "Pancho Villa is still in his cave. He's all alone and he's waiting for us."

"How do you know?" Pepe barked.

Lola and Dolores exchanged a look.

"Chili told us," Dolores said. The mention of Chili brought a spark to her eye, a faint spark, but still a glimmer that had otherwise all but disappeared. "Pancho Villa needs our help more than ever. He's losing faith that he can still lead the Mexican people. He doesn't know that Mexico still needs his leadership. We must help Pancho Villa so that he'll stop feeling sorry for himself and come back down the mountain!"

By now Dolores had become a different dog, just as she had when she first proclaimed that finding Pancho Villa was the Chihuahua's destiny that the ancient dogs had predicted when they had lived among the Aztecs. She jumped onto a rock and held her head high. Lola's heart swelled at the sight. Maybe Dolores could make the journey after all. Lola wanted more than anything to believe that Dolores could survive the climb to the top.

The dogs had walked all day and a cloud of feverish exhaustion now hovered above them. Lola knew she needed to find water and quick. As the dogs rested beneath a giant agave, Maxi took off on a scout. Minutes later, he came running back.

"A *pueblo* lies straight ahead," he barked.

A *pueblo*! The words set off a murmur of excitement among the dogs.

"We can find water at a *pueblo*," said Bombom, his dry tongue hanging almost to his chest.

"Or a tailor to wash and fix our dresses," said Bambi.

Indeed, Clarita and Bambi's dresses had become more stained and torn throughout the long day. As much as they tried, they just could not keep the desert dust from coloring their frocks a dull gray.

"We'll have to be careful," Lola said. "But hopefully we can find the water buckets left out for the goats and pigs. Or maybe it's wash day and the women will have filled the washing pools."

"Oh, I do hope it's wash day," Bambi yapped. "I'll feel so much better about everything when our dresses are clean."

"I'd like to bathe as well and have someone trim my nails," Clarita said.

"Hold on," Maxi said in a shaky voice. "A funny feeling is turning through my belly. Something about that *pueblo* seems . . . familiar."

"Have you been here before with your master?" Lola asked.

Maxi shook his big black head.

"Watch out!" Joaquín barked. "Someone's coming."

A boy had climbed through the rocks and agave and he suddenly stood in front of them, holding a rock over his head. The boy was long and skinny with curly black hair and thick black eyelashes fringing his almond-shaped eyes. He wore short white pants and a simple white shirt and he scowled and shook the rock in his hand.

"Get out, wild dogs," he yelled, aiming the rock at Maxi's head. "You won't attack our *pueblo*."

The boy threw the rock and it missed Maxi's head by inches. The Chihuahuas launched into a barking frenzy. Even Dolores was barking at full throttle. The noise was deafening. The boy picked up another rock from the ground and Maxi cowered. Without a thought, Lola and Joaquín went for the boy, biting his ankles with all the force they could muster. The boy let out a terrible scream and dropped the rock. Pandemonium broke out.

The dogs began jumping into the air, yipping and yapping and baring their teeth.

In the middle of this commotion, a big black dog, foaming at the mouth, came charging through the rocks and agave.

"Get back," the dog barked. "Get off my master."

"He started it," Clarita yapped hysterically.

The new dog zeroed in on Maxi, who was just about his size. "You wanna fight," the dog barked. "I'll give you dogs something to fight about."

Maxi let out a terrible, low growl and began to circle the threatening dog. All at once, as if on cue, the Chihuahuas stopped barking and stared because something very strange had happened. It was as if there were two Maxis. Maxi stopped his circling and stared. Even the boy stopped and stared.

Maxi and the new dog looked exactly alike.

Both dogs were big with black shaggy coats, pointy noses, and coal-black eyes. Both dogs had big furry paws and a long furry tail that reached to the ground.

"Do I know you?" Maxi said slowly.

No one said anything for a long moment until the boy jumped up, as if bitten once again by the dogs.

"The other puppy," the boy yelled out, ignoring his bloody ankle.

The new dog dropped his head to one side and looked quizzically at Maxi.

The boy continued, "Rosita had three puppies. I was only six years old, but I remember three puppies born in the straw. One puppy died. Couldn't breathe. Then we had two little black puppies, and I loved them so dearly. They followed me everywhere and we played all day. Until that man came riding through on his horse and told Papá he wanted one. Papá gave the puppy to the man for a few *pesos*. Mamá was so happy but I cried and cried. Oh, how could Papá sell little Bollo for a few *pesos*?" The boy began crying, tears streaming through his thick eyelashes and down his cheeks.

Maxi looked shocked. "I'm Bollo?"

"Bollo? My long lost brother Bollo?"

The noses of both dogs began quivering. Their whiskers trembled.

"I thought the *pueblo* seemed familiar," Maxi finally said. "I do remember now: my master put me into his jacket and I was bundled against his warm chest and we rode on his horse and I was scared and sad to be leaving my family and going far away with this man I didn't know. But now I've found you, my brother."

"I love happy endings," barked Clarita, jumping up and down. "You know the best part of this whole thing? Now Mommy and I each have our own dog to ride as we travel to the top of the mountain to tell Pancho Villa what we think of him. I call Maxi, Mommy, and you can have the other."

"Wait a minute, Clarita," Bambi said. "Maybe I should ride on Maxi, but we must implore this new dog to be more careful than Maxi was yesterday, when he threw us to the ground."

"Stop chattering, foolish dogs" Lola barked. "This dog may not want to come with us. What's your name, big dog?"

Before the dog could answer, the boy with the bloody ankle began waving his skinny arms. "Shoo," he said. "Get out, little wild dogs."

Despite finding his *pueblo* and his long lost brother, Maxi still knew his first line of duty. He stepped in front of the huddled group of Chihuahuas and growled, not scarily, but just enough to let the boy know he would protect the Chihuahuas.

"So these are your friends. Well, I won't hurt them." The boy stared at the dogs in deep thought. "You know, I haven't seen a pack of little wild dogs like you for a long time," he finally said. "Not like when I was little, when I'd watch what seemed like hundreds running across the sand. You're sort of a sorry-looking bunch—and those tiny things in dresses?" The boy slapped his thigh and began roaring with laugher. "Now I've seen everything!"

"Well, I've never been so insulted in all my life," Bambi said, turning away and sticking her nose in the air.

The boy turned to Maxi's brother and said, "Fidel, tell them to follow me and I'll give them some water. That old one looks like she might fall over any minute."

"Moisés is a good master," the big black dog named Fidel told the pack. "He won't harm you. Come."

And so, with Maxi and Fidel in the lead, the dogs started toward the *pueblo*.

FIFTEEN

The pack nervously made its way toward the *pueblo*.

"I'm scared," said Bombom, walking slowly with his tail between his legs. "It's been a long day and the last thing I need is for some old *abuela* to chase me with a broom."

"Don't worry," said Fidel. "My master will keep you away from the villagers. He knows how some people feel about wild dogs."

"I'd gladly be chased with a broom for the smallest drink of water," said Nini. "I'm so thirsty."

"Me too," said Pedro. "My throat is drier than a lizard's belly."

Lola knew the dogs were hurting to be complaining so much. Chihuahuas don't need a lot of water—a little drink and they are set for a two-day walk in the sun. Years of desert living had turned them into little camels.

"Remember the spring we found and how we all drank as much water as we wanted?" said Pepe. "Remember how cool and wet and wonderful the water was; how we drank and drank until the water sloshed in our bellies."

Memories of the cool spring filled the dogs' heads and they walked a little more quickly, thinking perhaps they would find that the oasis had miraculously moved to the *pueblo*.

The boy Moisés strode ahead, swinging his long arms and whistling a tune. He led the dogs along the edge of the tiny *pueblo* toward an adobe hut. He went around back to a small patch of land enclosed by a wood gate. Here he gathered together several beaten tin pans that were stacked on a table, and he filled them with water from a pitcher. With a wide smile, Moisés set the pans of water on the dirt. The dogs fell upon the water and lapped up their long-awaited drink. The boy generously filled three tins so that all the dogs could drink at once without having to push and shove.

When the pans were emptied, the boy just laughed, filled them again, and set them down. Again, the dogs drank every drop. One more time, the boy filled the pans and set them down.

"Take it easy," Moisés laughed.

The boy knelt down and began petting Maxi from the top of his head down his back. Over and over the boy's hand stroked Maxi's black coat. Lola stared. Maxi didn't flinch or try to move away. In fact, he lifted his head and smiled, a big goofy grin that spread from ear to ear.

Strange feelings gripped Lola. All at once, she wanted to bite the boy's hand so that he would stop petting Maxi; at the same time, she wanted Moisés to pet her. Did it feel good to have a human touch you like that? If not, why did Maxi look so happy?

"Brother Bollo, I can't believe you've come back," Fidel said, as he sat beside Maxi. "I'm sorry you were sold to that man. How many times I wished it was me who'd left that day. Where did you go? Was it terrible?"

"No, Brother Fidel, I had a good master who loved me and taught me how to obey. He took me riding and hunting with him, and he said I was his best friend ever. No dog ever wants to lose the master who calls him his best friend. I know that *pueblo* people don't like the *hacendados*, but they aren't all bad."

"And now that you've returned, you'll never leave again, right?"

Maxi looked around; the entire pack was staring at him, waiting to hear his answer. Would he leave the dogs in the middle of their journey? Most every dog had the same thought—*Don't leave, Maxi! We will never make it without you.*

"You guarded the pack at night, Maxi, and you told me why some dogs like humans," Lola said softly.

"You carried me from the burning house and saved me," said Dolores.

"You told me to jump in the fountain at the *hacienda* when my tail was burning. I was panicking and didn't know what to do. I might have burned to a crisp," said Manny.

"You gave everyone sausage from the long string that you took out of the kitchen, and you gave me the biggest piece," said Bombom.

"You let us ride on your back ever since we left the *hacienda*," said Bambi.

"You got our dresses dirty because you weren't being careful when Hawk swooped down to get us, but you did save us," said Clarita. "Still, my dress got dirty . . . but I forgive you."

Maxi looked at the pack. He opened his mouth to speak, but before his words could form, a clap of thunder filled the air.

"What's that noise?" shouted Moisés.

The thunder grew louder and stronger and the dogs began coughing and choking from the thick cloud of dust that blew in.

"Horses," shouted Moisés. "Cowboys on horses." He ran out into the road beside the yard and shouted, "Fidel, Bollo, come with me! Tell the other dogs to hide."

No one had to tell the other dogs to hide because they were already under the table, huddled behind some wooden crates, their little knees knocking. Only Lola and Bombom followed behind Fidel and Maxi.

But the dogs could hardly see the ground before them, so terrible was this dust storm that overtook the road. The thundering noise filled their ears and rumbled through their bodies.

Human voices began to fill the air:

"What's happening?"

"Mamá, Papá, I'm scared!"

"Run away, run away!"

Lola and Bombom narrowly missed being kicked by frantic feet running along the road. The thundering came closer and soon a hundred hooves ran past the dogs. Then a hoof landed on the end of Lola's tail, sending a searing pain through her body to her nose.

"Bombom, come here or you'll be trampled," barked Lola, who now pressed her body into a doorway and wrapped her sore tail between her legs. Bombom pressed close beside her.

I'm so glad I'm small, she thought, but she worried about Fidel and Maxi. Where had they gone? For several moments, the thundering of hooves continued to torment Lola and Bombom as they pressed against the doorway, but then the thundering faded, and, finally, it stopped.

Lola and Bombom peeked out of the doorway and looked down the path that led to the *pueblo*'s *zócalo*. The *zócalo* was now filled with men on horses—strange men, white men, young men—and the villagers were huddled around, staring at these invaders.

Lola and Bombom moved closer until they were right on the *zócalo*'s edge. Hiding behind a basket that someone had dropped in the excitement, they watched as a man took a gun from his holster and fired two shots in the air. The people shrieked.

"Do you know who I am?" The man called out. He wore a green shirt and a wide-brimmed hat that shaded his white skin.

The terrified villagers said nothing.

"I'm Lieutenant George Patton and these are my men from the United States Cavalry. Say hello, boys."

The boys shouted out, "Hello!"

The villagers said nothing. The white-faced men were speaking words they could not understand. The lieutenant pointed to an Indian sitting on a horse beside him. "Tell them what I said," he told him.

The Indian spoke to the villagers. The villagers nodded.

"I'm here looking for a wanted man," Lieutenant Patton continued in his booming voice. "I'm looking for Pancho Villa and you'd better tell me straight off if you've seen him because I'll be plenty mad if you don't."

The Indian spoke; the villagers stared blankly. But at the mention of Pancho Villa, Lola's ears pricked up. What did this boorish man want with Pancho Villa?

"I'm here because my boss, General John Pershing, sent me, and the general's here, in this godforsaken country, because his boss sent him. Do you know of his boss?"

The Indian spoke to the villagers and a few nodded.

"His boss is Woodrow Wilson, the president of the United States of America, and he wants us to find Pancho Villa, dead or alive. You think he's a hero but he's a murderous bandit and we're going to find him. Thousands of American soldiers are combing the entire state of Chihuahua and we won't leave until we hunt him down. Now, if he's hiding in this village of yours, if he's in one of your tiny houses, locked in a closet, you'd better tell me now and save yourselves a lot of trouble."

SIXTEEN

Somewhere off in the distance a baby cried and a donkey brayed. Lola and Bombom moved down the path closer toward the white-faced men on their horses.

Was Pancho Villa really hiding in this *pueblo*—locked in a closet?

How could Pancho Villa be hiding in a closet when he was most certainly at the top of the Sierra Madre Mountains?

What if Chili and Dolores were wrong? What if Crow had tricked them?

What if Pancho Villa was hiding in the *pueblo*, in a closet, and the white-faced men found him?

What if Lola never had the chance to be held by Pancho Villa so that his power seeped into her fur and she could become a stronger leader and save the Chihuahuas?

The villagers gazed silently at this Patton man. The dark faces stared at the white faces and the white faces stared back.

A man stepped forward from within the crowd. He walked tall and proud toward the Patton man and stopped right in front of his horse. Lifting his straw hat from his head and placing it over his heart, he said, "You are free to look for Pancho Villa in all our closets if you like. You can look under our beds too. If the great fighter is hiding here, I'd like to know, because I sleep upon a straw mat on the dirt, and I don't have a closet."

The Patton man chuckled. "Who are you?"

"My name is Manuel and I am the *pueblo* counsel."

"Tell me, Manuel, has Pancho Villa and his revolution done you any favors? Is your village richer? Do you have more food? I look around and I see your people don't wear shoes. How many men have left to fight with Pancho Villa, never to return? How many women are widows; how many children are orphans?

The counsel held a steady gaze. His worn pants, frayed at the hems and dirty on the seat, were held up by a length of rope tied around his waist. He wore no shoes.

"We can't deny that death and hardship have gripped our *pueblo*," Manuel said. "But so has thievery, such as the taking of our land by *hacienda* owners. This *pueblo* was once surrounded by land that belonged not to me, and not to another man, but to our entire *pueblo*, and we cared for this land and in return it gave the gift of abundant corn, beans, and peppers. And when our time is finished, our sons and daughters should be the ones to care for and harvest this land, and then their sons and daughters."

Lola noticed how the villagers all stood a little taller as Manuel continued to speak.

"We have tended this land for centuries, but it was stolen from us," Manuel said. "We could survive only by working for the rich men who made *pesos* off our labor; we work like slaves on the land that was once our mother."

Lola crept along the path, closer and closer she skulked. She had to see the face of this man who spoke so fearlessly to the white-faced man on the big horse. The closer she came to the white-faced man, the more she smelled his hot anger, wafting from his heated chest.

"Tell me, *Señor* Manuel, if Pancho Villa isn't under your bed or in your closet, he must be in those mountains. I imagine you know those mountains well, probably have explored every cave and crevice. I'll pay you one hundred American dollars to take me into those mountains and show me where your hero Pancho Villa might be hiding. Have you had one hundred dollars before? That money would buy a lot of shoes and food for your orphans. Tell me, is that boy an orphan?" The white-faced Patton man pointed right at Moisés, who was standing right behind Manuel.

For the first time, Manuel's body stiffened; his deepening anxiety filled Lola with dread. "This boy is my son."

"Maybe your son would like to be our guide into the mountains. I'll pay him two hundred, but we're leaving right now."

"No, my son stays here," Manuel said firmly, shielding Moisés's skinny body with his own.

The growing tension proved too much for Fidel, who moved to Manuel's side and snarled. The hair on Lola's back began to rise. The white-faced man Patton put his hand on his gun and every man behind him did the same.

"You better quiet down that dog," he said.

Lola froze. Would Fidel bark and would the white-faced man shoot him?

Laughter broke through the heavy, tense silence.

Who dared to laugh? Lola wondered. The Patton man rocked in his saddle, a deep laugh erupting into the cooling air.

"Suit yourself, *campesino.* It's not every day you could make one hundred cold American cash. Let's go, men."

With that, the white-faced Patton turned his horse around and rode out of the *pueblo*, with all his men thundering behind. As quickly as they arrived, they left, leaving a cloud of dust in their wake.

"Good boy," Manuel murmured, putting a hand upon Fidel's back before taking Moisés in his arms and hugging him close. Fidel turned and looked at the father and son with an adoring gaze and once again that funny feeling squeezed in Lola's chest.

The villagers began talking excitedly, waving their hands and shaking their heads.

"No *gringo's* going to stop the Revolution," one young man shouted to another. "*Tierra y Libertad*—Land and Freedom! The land is for those who work it."

"*Viva* Pancho Villa!" an old man cried into the sky.

"*Viva* Mexico!" trilled a woman with a long black braid wrapped around her head. She picked up her skirt and began turning in a circle, faster and faster, her red skirt swirling about her body like a trail of blood. A burly man with a guitar began strumming a tune. He sang:

In the north lives Villa

In the south lives Zapata

What I want is revenge

For the death of Madero

As the woman danced to the guitar, Lola turned and, with Bombom by her side, she ran back to find the other dogs.

SEVENTEEN

Lola and Bombom found the dogs still huddled together beneath the wood table in the little fenced area behind Moisés's house.

"What happened," they all clamored, charging out from under the table. Lola noticed that Dolores came last, crawling through the dirt with great difficulty.

"That white-faced man wants Pancho Villa," said Lola. "He's going into the mountains right now to find him."

"Well, pooh to Pancho Villa," said Bambi, lying down and crossing her front legs.

"I agree," said Joaquín, his eyes looking beady in the darkening night. "This whole quest to find Pancho Villa is getting out of hand, don't you think? Now that those men are on their way, why don't we take it easy and relax in this *pueblo* for a few days. There's plenty of water to go around."

"No," Lola barked forcefully. "That man wants to capture Pancho Villa. Our journey is more important than ever."

"Come now," Joaquín said. "Who really wants to climb up that steep, dangerous mountain and risk a run-in with those foul men when we could stay here?"

"I do," said Dolores.

Joaquín's eyes filled with pity. "You, old dog, are the last one who should climb that mountain. You can barely walk anymore. Why throw away the little time you have left on a treacherous journey that will lead nowhere."

Dolores lifted her head. "I'm going up the mountain with Lola. Who else is coming?"

The other dogs remained silent, looking from Dolores to Joaquín to Lola.

"Well, I don't want to go, but staying here isn't much of an option. This house is so small, I don't know where we'd sleep," said Clarita, looking around with a frown.

"You'd sleep in the yard," someone said. It was Fidel, who had returned to join the group with Maxi by his side.

"Sleep outside?" Clarita's eyes bugged from her head. "It's one thing if you're a wild dog, but a kept dog?"

"Yes, and you eat when there's food, and you don't when there isn't, which is pretty often. Some days I'm thrown only an old tortilla. The Revolution fighting have left our *pueblo* poorer than ever, and we've lost half of our men, our fathers and brothers. The life of a *pueblo* dog is not the same as that of a *hacienda* dog."

"I'm sorry, brother," said Maxi, dropping his black head.

"It's not your fault you were taken," Fidel said. "But I hope you stay. I know you feel responsible for these dogs, but I'd be happy until my dying day if I had my brother back."

"You have to stay." Bambi had jumped to her feet and was wagging her tail with great excitement. "You've found your long lost brother, and what's more important than family? I'd be lost without my darling Clarita. She's the light of my life, my one joy."

"Oh, mommy, we're so lucky to have one another," Clarita said. "We're so lucky we were raised to be ladies, not like these unfortunate wild dogs, and some day we'll wear beautiful dresses again. You can take the dog out of the *hacienda*, but you can't take the *hacienda* out of the dog. Isn't that right?"

"Yes, Clarita, you're absolutely right." Bambi went to Clarita's side and began licking her face with her tongue.

"We must leave now," Lola said, pacing around the small yard. "If we wait until morning, the white-faced men on their big horses may have already found Pancho Villa's cave."

"But night is falling. How can we get to the mountains in the stinkin' dark," said Pedro. "Better wait until morning, when the sun can be our guide."

Lola's heart was racing and her nerves jumping. How could the other dogs sit still? She wanted to run out of the yard, away from the *pueblo*, across the desert, and to the top of the mountains without stopping for a second. If only she could, but she had to take care of her pack before anything, even before saving Pancho Villa. But the white-faced men weren't waiting until morning.

"If we don't leave now, we might lose our chance to ever find Pancho Villa," she finally said. "Doesn't anyone care that we've come so far and now those strange-speaking men might get to Pancho Villa first? What happened to our quest to save the pack—to help Pancho Villa and perhaps all of Mexico?"

The dogs began to stir as they grappled with this thought.

Bambi spoke first. "I am not walking all that way to save Pancho Villa and Mexico, or to save this pack. I am going to give Pancho Villa a piece of my mind; I wouldn't want those *gringos* to get in the way of me telling Pancho Villa what I think of him."

She began trotting about with an angry look on her face. "I didn't come all this way for nothing. Pancho Villa is going to sit still and listen as I give him a piece of my mind. After all, he is responsible for our *hacienda* burning down. I don't care what anyone says—if he hadn't been born, it wouldn't have happened."

"It's not safe traveling at night when the coyotes are prowling," said Mela. "And how will we know where to go? That's a big mountain range. I mean, look at it!"

The dogs all turned toward the mountains. The sun had almost completely disappeared and just a wisp of light remained, just enough to illuminate the Sierra Madres, which filled the entire expanse of the horizon and reached almost all the way to the moon and the stars. In fact, it seemed if you stood at the highest mountain peak you could even touch the stars.

"How are we ever going to find Pancho Villa up there?" asked Nini in the tiniest voice.

Indeed staring at the massive mountain range, it seemed impossible that anyone could find a single man sitting in a cave; might as well search for a flea on a horse.

"You don't have to go," said Fidel. "It's not too late to change your minds."

"No!" Lola barked. "We Chihuahuas are courageous. We may be small, but we're mighty. Look how far we've come. We can't turn around now."

"You keep insisting on finding Pancho Villa. But I have a better offer," said Joaquín slyly as he skulked around the pack. "Stay here with me, dogs. We'll get a good night's rest and tomorrow we'll go back toward Chihuahua City. Remember that time we lived for a spell on the outskirts of town, near that spot where the people dumped their trash? We found old tortillas and even part of a pig's head once. What fun we had!"

"Yeah, until that man chased us with his *machete*," said Manny with a scowl. "He almost got my ear."

"Who wants to go?" Joaquín continued. "Mela? Nini? Pedro? Tell me, do we really expect to find Pancho Villa up there?"

"I'm going with Lola," said Dolores. "I've never felt more sure of anything. My destiny is to walk up that mountain."

"Me too," said Bombom.

"I'm not going anywhere without Lola," said Mela.

"Good luck making your way to the mountain trail with Dolores, Bambi and Clarita," said Joaquín. "Do you really think they can make it across the desert to the mountain trail?"

Lola said nothing, but she knew Joaquín was right. What was she thinking?

"We can help," said Fidel.

"How?" asked Lola.

"Maxi can take Bambi and Clarita, and I'll carry Dolores. We can run with you through the desert and bring you to the bottom of the best trail to the mountaintop. The white-faced men on big horses will spend a lot of time winding round and round the mountain on the main trail. This other path is steeper but it gets you to the top much faster. It's the path that Moisés takes when he goes into the mountains. Also, it's best that Maxi and I come along because the coyotes won't attack if we are protecting you."

"Well then, I guess I'll go to Chihuahua City myself and eat the entire pig head," Joaquín said angrily.

"You don't know for sure that there is a pig head, and if you travel alone at night, you'll surely be taken by a coyote," said Maxi with such a patient tone that Lola thought he truly might be a saint. "Let's go, everyone. No one's staying behind!"

So Maxi crouched low to the ground and Bambi and Clarita climbed on his back, and Fidel crouched down and Dolores climbed on his, and the dogs began running through the desert, not so fast that they would tire quickly, but at a brisk pace that allowed them all to run together toward the Sierra Madre mountain range.

The dogs ran through the desert night, through the cool air, with the stars twinkling above.

EIGHTEEN

After two hours of running, the dogs came to the base of the mountains and collapsed in a heap.

"I've never, ever worked so hard," whimpered Clarita as she slid off Maxi's back.

"But you didn't run a step," said Mela, panting so hard she could hardly choke out the words.

"It's not so easy to hold on to Maxi; you try it some time."

"Believe me, I wish I could," Pepe muttered, fed up to the tip of his ears with Clarita's spoiled attitude.

Fidel had gently lowered himself to the ground so that Dolores could slide from his back. "You've safely made it across the desert without losing any dogs to coyotes, but now you have new dangers to beware," he said to Lola gravely. "The mountains are filled with gray wolves, and they are fierce and savage. And you might not find such easy places to hide as you would on the desert floor. You've never been in the mountains before?"

"We've never come across the desert this far before," said Lola, suddenly realizing the feat that she had accomplished. She had brought her entire pack all this way, even old Dolores.

"It's different from the desert," said Maxi. "It's really quite beautiful. If the gray wolves don't get you, you should really enjoy your journey."

Fidel began pacing. "We should return to our *pueblo* before Moisés gets worried. He may assume that we're off carousing as brothers, but I don't want him to venture out on his own looking for us. You know how foolish boys can be."

The dogs all dropped their heads and stared at the ground. The moment they had all been dreading had come. No one wanted Fidel and Maxi to leave, not just because they would lose their bodyguards, but also because they loved the kind and generous brothers with all their hearts.

"*Adiós*, Maxi," Lola said, voicing what no other dog could manage to say. "We'll never forget you, ever. We owe you our lives, and this journey belongs to you as well."

"You're the best wild dogs I've ever known," Maxi said, looking at Lola with sad eyes. "I hope you find Pancho Villa, Lola. And I hope you discover why man and dog can be the best of friends. I hope that Pancho Villa shows you the kindness that some men give to dogs."

With that, Fidel and Maxi turned and galloped off into the desert, back toward their *pueblo* and their master, to live the rest of their lives together as brothers.

NINETEEN

With Lola in the lead, the dogs began walking along the mountain trail. Slowly and steadily they climbed up the mountain.

"It's different here," said Manny. "I've never seen so many trees."

"Packs of trees," said Pedro. "One stinkin' tree after the next. And such tall trees with so many stinkin' green leaves."

"Tall skinny trees with skinny leaves. And big fat trees with fat leaves. I've never seen anything like this in the desert," said Bombom.

"And the air—it's so cool," said Nini.

"Where are we, Lola?" said Pepe. "How come we've never been here before?"

"Because we're desert dogs, not mountain dogs," said Lola as she gazed upward toward the towering trees that tickled the sky. "But it's wondrous, isn't it."

For some time the dogs walked along the mountain trail, gawking at the trees, which seemed to grow taller and taller with every turn of the winding trail, their many strong limbs outstretched to the sky. Monarch butterflies flew here and there, landing on the delicate flowers that nestled in the moss beneath the trees. Yellow flowers, pink flowers, blue flowers. There wasn't a single cactus anywhere.

Just as the morning began warming, Lola noticed Dolores wobbling on her legs as her eyes began rolling back in her head.

"What is it, Dolores?" Lola asked with alarm.

"Lola, you must admit I did pretty well for an old dog," Dolores said as her knees buckled and her body swayed. "I never thought I'd make it to the oasis. Then I never thought I'd make it to the *hacienda*. Never in a million years did I imagine I'd get to the *pueblo*. And now I'm walking in these beautiful mountains. Something bigger than my old and aching body was certainly pulling me along."

"What are you talking about," Lola whimpered as she watched Dolores fall.

"Remember that I tried to live my life with the same strength and grace as the Chihuahuas who lived in the Aztec temples," Dolores somehow managed to say as she lay on her side. "Even if the other dogs didn't always care to hear the stories of their ancient ancestors, perhaps I've served as a model of their spirit. If so, then I haven't lived my life in vain."

Dolores closed her eyes. The dogs all gathered around. They glanced at each other nervously and wondered what to do.

"Let's go," said Joaquín. "She's as good as dead. Why waste time standing around?"

"She's not dead," said Lola angrily. "We can't just leave her for the . . ."

"The gray wolves? Oh, I'm sure they'll be back," said Joaquín.

As the dogs argued, a warm, peaceful feeling washed over Dolores. Here she was, lying on the ground, probably breathing her last breath, and she felt light as a feather and positively elated. Her eyes flickered. A swirl of dust rose up. *Why, it's Chili*, she thought happily, so glad to once again see her old friend. She opened her mouth to call his name but not a sound came out.

"Dolores, it's me, Lola. Can you get up?"

"Why would I want to get up?" Dolores whispered. Lying in the dirt, she was the most comfortable she had ever been.

"We can't leave you here, Dolores," Lola continued, her voice wavering. "You need to get up so that we can find somewhere safe for you to rest. The sun is too hot, the steep mountain trail . . ."

"She's dead," barked Joaquín with great exasperation. "Who's coming with me? I'll take you up the mountain if Lola's going to hang around here as Dolores goes stiff. Soon as the gray wolves get a whiff of new death, though, they'll be running in for their morning snack. I don't want to be here when that happens."

"Can't we at least pull her off the trail?" asked Mela.

"She needs a proper burial," said Bambi with great indignation, her tail twitching from side to side. "We need to call the priest. If *Señora* Terrazas were here she'd be making all the arrangements. How many funerals I've watched her plan."

"Mommy, I don't have my black mourning gown," cried Clarita. "The last time I wore it was to *Señora* Terrazas's brother's funeral. Remember how we sat by the coffin on those black satin pillows. Wherever will we find a black satin pillow around here?"

With that, Clarita began to cry, releasing big, loud, terrible sobs as if the funeral were for her own mother.

"Now, now, it's not as bad as all that," a voice said.

"It's not?" asked Bombom. "Wait, who said that?"

Who said that indeed. Lola sat up straight and looked around, half expecting to see a jesting gray wolf, licking his chops. Instead she saw a Chihuahua coming down the trail, a Chihuahua with such a confident and supreme air that Lola remained still as the dog approached the pack. The dog went straight over to Dolores's side and licked her face. As she licked Dolores, the other dogs gaped, looking from this new dog to Dolores and back again. The Chihuahua with her graceful manner and long, golden coat, looked similar to Dolores. She too had white tufts of fur on her chest and amber brown eyes. Dolores was clearly much older, but this new dog could have been her daughter, her beautiful daughter.

"Dolores, not to worry. You've arrived," the dog said softly.

Dolores opened her heavy lids. "An angel," she whispered to Chili. "Is this is the same angel that came to you? Have I really gone to heaven that quickly? I always imagined it would take longer, and I had always hoped you and I could go together."

"You're not going to heaven, Dolores," the new dog replied. "We're going to see *La Bruja*."

"What about the other dogs," Dolores said, in such a tiny voice, everyone leaned forward to hear her. "Are they going too?"

"We were mainly waiting for you, but we knew the entire pack would come as well," said the kind dog. "Don't worry. *La Bruja* is close. You'll soon have water and food."

Dolores pushed her eyes open again. "Who are you?"

"Josefina," the dog said.

"Chili's here too?"

"Oh, yes, Chili's here, and he has been most concerned. You dogs have really kept him busy. He worked hard to lead you to the oasis, to help you escape the burning *hacienda*, to bring you to us. At last, he too can rest and prepare for his own transition to the other side, to become a twinkling star above."

"What's going on?" Lola barked, finally finding her voice in the midst of this fantastic development. Her heart soared as she realized Dolores was not dead, but her head spun with the intrusion of this new dog. "Who are you? Where's Chili?'

A swirl of dust surrounded the dogs. "Chili's here with us," Josefina said, still licking Dolores's face, eyes, and ears. "Are you ready to go to my home? I'll explain everything after you drink some water and get some rest."

"Oh, I'd love a stinkin' drink of water," said Pedro.

"Me too," echoed Manny, Pepe, and Nini.

"Come along then," said Josefina, turning and walking back down the trail.

At Josefina's command, Dolores miraculously stood up and shook her head. She began following Josefina, and Lola walked alongside Dolores, not willing to let this new dog take full control. All the other dogs followed behind. The dogs climbed the trail, even higher into the mountains. Lola marveled at how Dolores, just inches from death moments ago, had sprung back to life. She moved along with renewed purpose.

Suddenly, Josefina veered off the trail and took the dogs into a forest, the likes of which they had never seen. Thick columns of pine trees towered toward the sky. The trees were clustered so closely together that only patches of blue sky peaked through. The dogs began padding through a thick floor of pine needles that sometimes pricked their paws.

"I've never seen so many trees ever," whispered Bombom.

"And birds, do you hear the birds? They're chirping in ways I've never heard," said Mela. "Singing songs I've never heard. These must be mountain birds, not desert birds. Everything here's so different."

"The air is so fresh and smells like trees," said Nini. "But what I don't understand is why it's cooler up here when we're closer to the sun. We should be burning up since we're closer!"

TWENTY

"I've known about the packs of Chihuahuas on the desert floor, but I've never actually met any before," Josefina said as the dogs padded along through the pine forest.

"You've never been part of a pack?" Lola asked with disbelief.

"Oh, no, it's just been me and my family on this mountain for my entire life. My husband, José, my mother and father, my sister, and my *abuelo* and *abuela* before that."

"Where are they all now?"

"All gone, except for me and José. But not for long. We're expecting puppies."

"I thought you looked fat," Clarita said. "But puppies—I adore puppies!"

"Yes, puppies are a blessing," Dolores said. "But it must have been difficult for you and your husband all alone."

The dogs all looked sadly at Josefina. Everyone knows that Chihuahuas do not like to be alone.

"It's okay," Josefina said with a smile. "We have our companion, and though she's human, she's kind of like a dog."

Lola noticed that Josefina did not call her human "master" or act as if the human were in charge of her.

"But tell me about your pack," Josefina continued with genuine interest.

"Our pack was once big and strong," Lola said. "My *padre* Cuauhtémoc led the pack for ten years and once we had one hundred dogs. But now it's just us."

Lola looked around at her bedraggled dogs and felt a tug at her heart. What troopers they had been, coming along on this long, hard journey and hardly complaining. The dogs had really dug down deep inside and discovered their own strength and bravery.

Even Bambi and Clarita, Lola had to admit, had stopped complaining so much and had toughened up. Here they both were, walking through the pine forest, without Maxi's help, and they actually looked to be enjoying themselves.

"Used to be we'd run across another pack every now and then, but we haven't seen any other Chihuahuas for a long time," said Bombom wistfully.

"There's not many packs left," said Josefina. "You're definitely among the last. In fact, you may be the very last pack of wild Chihuahuas."

The dogs all stopped beneath a pine tree and looked at one another with startled expressions. The very last pack of wild Chihuahuas?! How could that be when once hundreds, perhaps thousands, ran wild through the desert?

"Wild Chihuahuas once ruled the desert. What happened?" asked Lola.

"Sadly, the wild Chihuahuas are a dying breed," Josefina said quietly. "It's a tough life, living in the harsh desert, and the Revolution has only made things harder. Who's to say what will happen to Chihuahuas in the future. What kind of lives will we lead? We're really not like other dogs and I hope we find our place in the world. But enough sad talk. I'm just glad you found your way and brought Dolores. I'm so delighted to meet you all." Josefina turned and gazed lovingly at every single dog, even Joaquín.

"How did you know we were coming?" asked Dolores.

"Chili told me."

"Ah, of course. But how?"

Josefina then told the dogs about how Chili began appearing in her dreams three nights earlier. "In the first dream, an old gray dog sat upon a rock and described how a pack of wild Chihuahuas was on their way to see me, and how they would be bringing a special Chihuahua named Dolores," Josefina said. "I was confused by the dream, so I told *La Bruja*. Luckily, *La Bruja* is used to getting messages through dreams, and she told me to ask the old dog to return to my dreams and bring more information."

So before Josefina went to sleep the next night, she asked the dog to come back. And, indeed, that night Chili reappeared, sitting on the same rock and explaining that Dolores was one of the rare mystical dogs. He told Josephina that she was a mystic too, and it was time that she and Dolores should meet.

Josefina walked along with a spring in her step, obviously thrilled to be walking beside perhaps the only dog in all of Mexico just like her, one of the last of the mystics who had descended directly from Aztec Techichis.

"I was worried you'd never come, and I'd never meet Dolores, and my puppies would never hear any stories about their Techichi ancestors who lived with the Aztecs," Josefina said.

But each night, thanks to Chili, Josefina would see the daily happenings of the dogs. She dreamed of them drinking at the oasis and discovering the *hacienda*. She dreamed of Lola being stolen by Ramona and of the fire in the closet. The worst dream had been a nightmare, when the pack was eating inside the kitchen of the burning *hacienda*.

"Run away, stop eating *lengua*," she had whimpered.

All along, she dreamed, as Hawk tried to steal Clarita, and when Maxi found Fidel at Moises's *pueblo*. Josefina had dreamed as Joaquín tried to steal away the pack from Lola over and over again. What Josefina knew for sure was that Lola was a brave leader and that the dogs had made it to the mountains because of her smarts, courage, and determination. They would have never made it anywhere with Joaquín in charge.

"When you arrive at the cave of *La Bruja,* you will be our honored guests," she said to all the dogs.

"This human won't chase us with sticks and brooms?" asked Nini, with worried eyes.

"Oh, no, she'll be pleased to see such a dignified pack of wild Chihuahuas."

They were a special pack, except for the bully with the chip on his shoulder. Josefina snuck a peek at Joaquín, who was trailing behind with his usual sneer on his face. In every pack, there was one of these bad-tempered dogs, suffering from a lack of self-esteem, feeling lousy about his size as some Chihuahuas do, and clearly jealous of Lola and the respect she commanded.

But what else? Something ugly troubled this dog.

The dogs continued on through the fragrant pine forest, entranced by the singing birds and the lacy sunlight drifting through the branches.

They came upon a stream, not a trickle of water as they might find in the desert, but a rushing stream, water flowing so fast the dogs became excited, and they stood on its banks and gazed at it with wagging tails.

"I've never seen so much stinkin' water in my entire life," exclaimed Pedro. "I didn't know the world had so much water!"

"Poor desert dogs. The mountains are filled with streams like this," said Josefina. "Follow me. I know a spot where we can safely cross over the stream."

Josefina led the pack further up the bank where a thick line of rocks formed a bridge from one side of the stream to the other. First, all the dogs took a long drink of the freshest, sweetest water they had ever tasted. They then began crossing the stream.

As the dogs walked across, the rushing water filled their ears and the water flew into their faces and they barked with glee.

"I love this stream," barked Nini, shaking off water droplets that tickled his fur.

"Mommy, it's like having a bath, and I haven't had a bath in so long and maybe it will make my dress a little more clean," said Clarita.

What little dress Clarita had left was just a thin scrap of fabric that hung around her skinny neck. The dress with its flounce was long gone, caught and torn on branches and rocks, shredded to pieces. But Bambi and Clarita hardly cared about their destroyed dresses anymore, so much did they enjoy the beauty of the day and the company of the other dogs. Lola had been noticing for the past two days that Bambi and Clarita seemed, well, truly happy, not complaining of anything.

"*Ah, it's a dog's life*," Lola thought as she jumped from rock to rock.

Once the dogs had all crossed the stream, they continued on a short way until they came to a clearing in the forest, a clearing ringed by the tallest, strongest pine trees on the entire mountain. Josefina led them to an enormous rock at one side of the clearing and within the rock was an opening to a cave.

Josefina barked a short, quick bark and a woman appeared from within the cave. At the same time, two bats flew out directly over the woman's grizzled head. She stood in the cave's opening and peered down on the dogs, all huddled together and peering back up at her.

The old woman was small but stout, her chest round as a barrel. She wore a heavy black cloak made of lamb's wool and a wooly black skirt wrapped around her thick waist and fastened with a length of rope. Two long silver braids hung down her back.

For a long time, the dogs and the woman exchanged looks, until finally, the woman released a wicked, jagged cackle that made all the dogs cower.

"What an utterly delightful, wonderfully exciting pleasure to meet you all," she cackled, hands on her round hips. Behind her monumental nose lay two black gleaming eyes, crow's eyes, and just above her liver-colored mouth three wiry black hairs protruded from a big black mole. She grabbed these three hairs and began twisting and pulling them as she regarded the dogs further. Her crow eyes sparkled when she met Dolores's gaze. She stooped down and picked up Dolores as if she had just found the long lost treasure of the Sierra Madres. Her thick calloused fingers began to comb through Dolores's matted hair ever so gently.

"At last, the special one we've been waiting for. Come Josefina, we will celebrate."

With that, Dolores looked up and licked *La Bruja's* monumental nose, as if finally meeting an old friend.

TWENTY-ONE

Josefina's husband, José, had the same long golden fur as his wife. He was, however, shy and quiet, unused to other dogs, but he politely greeted and welcomed them all. The Chihuahuas then lay down beneath the tallest pine in the circle of trees and settled in for a long afternoon's nap.

When they woke, *La Bruja* was busily stirring a stick through a big kettle that sat atop a ring of fire directly in the center of the clearing. Josefina and José lay on the ground beside her.

"We'll have a feast," she cried as the dogs came running toward the wonderful smell that wafted from the kettle. With rumbling bellies, the dogs began to beg, jumping up and down because the smell was so unbelievable delicious.

"Josefina, tell our guests to settle down and we'll eat presently," she cackled, because every word that came from *La Bruja*'s mouth came out as a cackle.

Whatever it was that *La Bruja* had cooked in her big, black, dented kettle tasted like heaven, as if sausage, pig ears, *lengua*, and plump mice had simmered in corn and *jalapeños* for an entire day, and the dogs ate and ate until they all fell to the ground in a stupor.

"Full Moon Stew gets them every time," *La Bruja* cackled, easing onto a tree stump that served as her stool and lifting Josefina onto her lap. A blue evening was beginning to descend on the clearing, causing *La Bruja* to squint at the dogs.

"I want to get to know you all," she continued, her rough hands stroking Josefina's beautiful long golden fur. "But first, I want to say *muchas gracias* for bringing Dolores." *La Bruja* looked down and smiled at Dolores who was sitting at her feet. "Poor Josefina was worried Dolores wouldn't get here in time to share her many important stories about the Techichis and the Aztecs. We must capture these stories before they're lost forever."

Two bats circled *La Bruja*'s head but she ignored them as she cast her crow's eyes over the dogs and stared at each one.

"Do you know who I am?" she asked the spellbound dogs.

The dogs shook their heads.

"I am *La Bruja*, a Rarámuri, and my people have lived in these mountains for hundreds of years, since the time of our brothers and sisters, the Aztecs. We used to live in the desert too, but when those Spanish *conquistadores* came and fought the Aztecs we moved further into the mountains to hide, and now we'll never leave. We brought several of the mystical Techichi with us into the mountains. This is where Dolores belongs."

The dogs nodded.

"But you're all on your way to find Pancho Villa who is hiding in one of the caves of Copper Canyon. I hope you find what you're looking for—although, I think some of you have already made great discoveries."

"Like what?" Mela asked.

"Mela, I think you've discovered you really want a master, just as Bambi and Clarita and Maxi had. I know for sure you'd like someone to give you a pretty dress to wear."

Mela nodded, brightening at the thought of a dress of her own.

"Oh, yes," chimed in Clarita, nodding in fierce agreement. "Mela would look just wonderful in green velvet with a red bow."

"Yes, Clarita, and you and your mother have discovered that an entirely different world exists outside of the *hacienda*, and you can live happily in that world too."

"Of course, *hacienda* life is the most desirable," Bambi said. "But Clarita and I are making the best of the situation."

"Pedro, Pepe, Manny, and Nini, you've all discovered how brave and strong you really are, and Bombom you've tested the depths of your loyalty to Lola."

At this moment, Lola thought *La Bruja* would skip over Joaquín. Who had anything nice to say about Joaquín? But instead *La Bruja* looked Joaquín squarely in the eye and called him to her side.

Lola waited for one of Joaquín's nasty retorts, but, instead, Joaquín meekly trotted over. As *La Bruja* bent over to pick up Joaquín, Josefina jumped off, making room for him to settle on *La Bruja*'s expansive lap. *La Bruja* began to run her hand over his fur, up and down, in a hypnotic fashion, still staring into his eyes.

"Your troubled heart is black," she said, plain and simple. "We must draw out the blackness so that you can enjoy your life. Tell me, little dog, from where did the blackness come from?"

Joaquín stared back at *La Bruja*, but this Joaquín was empty of his usual attitude and anger. Joaquín's eyes began to water and his nose began to twitch.

"Is the blackness why you want to steal the pack from Lola?" *La Bruja* asked. "Of course you can lead the pack if they decide you are a worthy leader with good intentions. But you don't seem interested in the good of the pack; you want something else. Tell me, Joaquín, why is your black heart obsessed with Lola?"

With that Joaquín began to blubber, words spilling from his mouth.

"*La Bruja*, I've been carrying an unbearable secret since a terrible day one year ago," Joaquín said, crouching on her wide lap, his sad head drooping into her skirt. "This secret is a heavy stone around my neck, and it pulls me deeper into my hatred for Lola with each passing day."

"What is it Joaquín?" asked *La Bruja*. "You are safe here. I won't let anyone hurt you. But if this is for Lola to hear, you must tell her."

Joaquín lifted his head, looked directly at Lola, and said, "I saw your *padre*, Cuauhtémoc, get bit by that rattlesnake who I knew had been lying in wait."

Sitting at *La Bruja*'s feet with the other dogs, Lola felt the sky crash down on her head; her heart began to pound fast and hard as a drum. "But no one was with him but me," she struggled to say because all the air had just whooshed out of her body.

Joaquín looked down at Lola from the safety of *La Bruja*'s lap. He shook his head and continued pushing the words from his throat where they'd been trapped for that long year. "I was there," he said. "I got up early that morning and was running around the rocks looking for lizards. I didn't have a mother or a father who would help me find food as you did. I was digging up some crickets when I saw the rattler in the rocks."

"What?" Lola shook her head in disbelief.

"I saw the snake beneath the rocks, saw her huge rattle, and I ran away. Then I saw you coming along with your *padre*, across the sand, and I hid behind a tumbleweed."

"But you didn't . . ."

The sky kept crashing down because of what young Joaquín did not do, what all the dogs were taught to do from the earliest age.

Joaquín's heavy shame lay thicker than the gray clouds that now clung to the blue evening mountains, but the shamefaced dog did not back down from telling his truth.

"No, I didn't warn you of the rattlesnake," Joaquín said. "I didn't bark out 'rattler' as I was supposed to. I saw you and your *padre* walking side by side and really crazy thoughts started crowding my head. How come I didn't have a father who took me on a morning walk? How come I had to find lizards all by myself? How come those coyotes had to take both my mother and father? They only took your mother but you still had your father and he loved you twice as much and everyone could see how much he loved you."

Joaquín was shaking like a dancing skeleton on *La Bruja*'s lap. She lay her hand on his back but he couldn't stop shaking.

"You didn't warn of us the rattler as we're taught to do," Lola said.

"I didn't see the baby," said Joaquín, still doing his skeleton dance.

As all the dogs knew, baby rattlesnakes are the most venomous, deadly, and dangerous. The baby snakes will eject all of their venom because they have not learned control yet, while adult snakes will eject only some of their venom some of the time.

"I wanted to hurt you, Lola. I hated you, walking along with your brave father. I thought it might bite you—of course, I didn't know for sure, but when the baby began to strike, your father jumped in its way to protect you. And that little devil bit Cuauhtémoc right by the heart. Your father was willing to die for you, Lola, and I didn't even have a father who could walk with me in the morning. I don't even remember my father."

The moments of that horrible morning came rushing back, and Lola could still see Cuauhtémoc falling to the ground and the rattlesnakes slithering away. Standing next to her fallen father, Lola howled in great pain, howled until Dolores and Chili came running, but it was too late to save her father. One moment, Lola had been walking along with her *padre*, the morning sun dancing on their fur, and the next moment he was dead in the dirt, and Lola's life, as well as every dog's in the pack, was forever changed.

Lola stared at Joaquín. "So Cuauhtémoc died because of you; but why do you hate me? Why have you made my life miserable?"

"That morning the entire pack surrounded you, took care of you because you lost your father and no one even noticed I was missing," answered Joaquín, his head hanging low.

"Just like when I lost my parents to those coyotes, no one worried about me. Everyone was upset about you and Cuauhtémoc losing your mother in that attack. I remember wandering around alone; I was so scared. You always got so much attention, and because you had so much, I hated you, Lola. When you became leader of the pack, I swore I would ruin your life like mine had been ruined."

"Oh, it's terrible," wailed Clarita, her tiny face scrunched in anguish. "I didn't know Joaquín was an orphan. No one told me. No wonder Joaquín's such a miserable soul and nobody likes him. I can't imagine my life without Mommy."

"It's just not right," said Bambi firmly.

"No, it wasn't right what happened," said Dolores, looking straight at Joaquín and sadly shaking her head. "We didn't know that you were behind the tumbleweed that terrible morning. But I can tell you, Joaquín, it wasn't really your fault that Cuauhtémoc died. You didn't see the baby rattler."

La Bruja's hand still rested on Joaquín's back. "Past is an old dead ghost," she said. "Mysterious world takes what it wants. This moment is a new day, a new beginning for Joaquín to rise again, and become the dog he wants to be."

La Bruja peered down her monumental nose at Joaquín, who looked back up with something in his eyes the other dogs had never before seen.

From what Lola could tell, it was a flicker of hope that warmed Joaquín's eyes.

La Bruja then waved her hand at Lola. "You, leader of the mighty little dogs, tell us, powerful one, how will you punish this dog who betrayed his pack?"

All the dogs turned to look at Lola. How would she punish Joaquín? Would she banish him from the pack, force him to walk back down the mountain alone and perhaps meet his fate in the jaws of a mountain lion? Or would she fight him?

"Come on, Lola, tear Joaquín apart," barked Manny. The dogs always loved a good fight.

The hurt in Lola's heart made her want to do both: fight him, then make him walk down the mountain alone, at night.

But at the same time, an idea came into Lola's head, an idea that seemed to belong to someone with a greater heart and more wisdom than she thought she had.

The idea seemed like it came from Cuauhtémoc. Lola did not know why this idea came into her head, and she did not have time to figure it out now, so she just spoke the idea, clear and firm.

"Joaquín belongs to our pack. He's one of us, and he's already paid his price by this long year of suffering," she said. "Having a black heart and violence in his mind is the worst punishment of all. As leader of the wild Chihuahuas, I say that Joaquín is now my *compadre*, to walk on one side while Bombom walks on the other. For as deeply as Joaquín was willing to tell his truth, I am now equally willing to trust him and seek his guidance and counsel as my co-leader of the wild Chihuahuas. Together, we'll take these dogs up the mountain to complete our journey."

Joaquín, his tail between his legs, gave Lola a look of complete disbelief. Then he dropped his head and looked to the ground. "I would be honored to lead the pack with you," he murmured. When he raised his head, Lola saw once again the flicker of hope in his eyes.

"Come then," Lola said. "You are to always remain by my side and serve as my eyes and ears and help the other dogs."

"With pleasure," said Joaquín, the smile on his face wrapped from ear to ear. And so as a terrible rainstorm can suddenly stop and the sun can appear, Joaquín changed from a mean and angry dog to a loving and gentle one.

It was a true miracle.

And in that moment, Lola and Joaquín turned their hate into a friendship that would last for the rest of their lives.

The next morning Lola rose with the sun and wandered about the clearing. *La Bruja* was already sweeping out her cave with a broom made of twigs, scritching, scratching in the dirt. Dolores and Josefina lay together on a patch of wool blanket beside the fire ring. Lola watched as they talked quietly together. In a short time, Lola would say goodbye to Dolores forever—dear, sweet Dolores who had cared for Lola almost her entire life, who believed she could be leader of the pack, and who remained steadfast by her side for this long journey. Lola lay in the dirt and rested her head on the ground. Feelings of loneliness washed over her like waves. How could she continue without Dolores?

"Dolores will always be in the most important place, in your heart," *La Bruja* said, squatting down beside Lola. "Don't worry. We'll take care of Dolores. She will be important to the puppies, the next generation. She will help them understand the stories, and who they are as mystical dogs, and when it's time for her to cross over, she won't be alone."

Lola peered into *La Bruja*'s sharp black eyes and was overwhelmed by a realization.

Suddenly, Lola remembered the day when Chili died, and when she saw Crow soaring back into the sky, higher and higher until he just about brushed the sun with his shiny black wings.

"I know where I've seen you before," Lola said. "You flew over the pack and told us that Pancho Villa was not dead after Coyote said he was. You told us you saw Pancho Villa in the Sierra Madres, living deep in a hill, in a dark and hidden place, and that he needed our help. It's because of you that we are here."

With that, *La Bruja* cackled, a rich, happy cackle. She stood up and went back to her sweeping, not saying another word.

Lola and her dogs gathered in the clearing. Bombom stood to Lola's right, Joaquín to her left, with Mela, Nini, Pedro, Pepe, Manny, Bambi, and Clarita close behind. The time had come to leave. "Goodbye, Josefina and José. Goodbye *La Bruja*," the dogs said in chorus.

And then came the moment that Lola had long dreaded. Lola went to Dolores and they touched noses. For a long moment, the two dogs kept their noses close.

"Thank you, Lola, for bringing me here," Dolores finally said.

"Dolores, I'll never forget you," Lola said, and she meant that never, ever, for a single second, would Dolores leave her heart and her mind.

"Of course you won't, Lola," Dolores said.

Now Josefina stood to one side of Dolores and *La Bruja* stood behind.

"You'd better hurry, because Pancho Villa is waiting and those white-faced men are catching up," cackled *La Bruja*.

"How will we know where his cave is?" Lola asked.

La Bruja cackled and pointed her fat finger at the top of the mountains. "He's up there somewhere. Good luck! When you see Pancho Villa, you tell him that he owes *La Bruja* a favor. He'll know what I mean."

Lola stole one last glance at Dolores before leaving. There she sat beside Josefina, serene as a queen, shimmering and glowing with her own special beauty. Lola could barely see the trail for the tears in her eyes.

TWENTY-TWO

This time, José led the dogs out of the clearing, back through the pine forest, across the stream, to a narrow mountain path that led straight up into the mountains.

"Pancho Villa is hiding somewhere in one of the caves inside one of those canyons," José said. The dogs all stared at the vast mountain. "If you stay on this trail and follow your noses, I know you'll find him," José added. "But follow your noses."

"Thank you, José, for showing us the way and for taking care of dear Dolores," Lola said solemnly.

"Oh, the pleasure is all mine." Without another word, José turned and scampered back into the pine forest.

Lola and the dogs set out, climbing the mountain trail that took them higher and higher into the mountains. The trail was steep and rocky and the dogs trudged along single file, not saying a word, just moving up the mountain with great determination, knowing they would not stop until they found Pancho Villa.

On and on the dogs trudged, up the steep mountain trail, winding round and round over rocky terrain as the trees grew even taller and skinnier. Several dogs began gasping as the air thinned. Looking over the trail into the deep canyons, their walls a coppery green, the dogs could see the blue ribbons of flowing rivers that wound through the deep canyons stretching off in all directions.

"Standing in the desert, looking at the mountains, I never imagined what it would be like to stand on the mountains and look at the desert," said Bombom.

"It's wonderful," said Manny, his tail wagging at the view.

Suddenly, the forest was filled with long shadows. Nightfall had come quickly, and Lola had not yet found a safe spot for the dogs to sleep. The forest, so beautiful and peaceful in the day, had turned dark and sinister. The tree branches seemed to claw angrily at the pitch-black sky.

We should be hiding by now, Lola thought with dread.

A sudden wind began to whip through the trees, shaking the angry branches into a furious frenzy. The wind was cold and icy and the dogs began to whimper.

"My eyes are blinded," barked Bombom as the wind slapped his face.

"I'm so scared, I want to go home," whimpered Clarita as the wind whirled around her teeny tiny, scrawny body. She leaned into the wind and tried to move forward but the wind pushed back with such a force, she tumbled and fell against her mother.

"Mommy, I want my warm bed. I want Maxi and Ramona," cried Clarita.

"We can't walk any further, Lola," Bambi pleaded. "It's too cold and dark."

"I'll find shelter," Lola barked over the howling wind, her heart pounding with fear. Why hadn't she found shelter while she still had light? The dogs had come so far and now they might be blown off the mountain.

Lola looked about wildly for a hiding place. She began running about the trees in a panic as the wind whipped even faster, swooshing and whooshing all around. There must be a hole in the ground, perhaps a thick bush....

"Who, who, who are you?"

What! Lola froze in her tracks. "Who said that?"

"Who, who, you dogs will be safe here!"

Lola looked up and noticed an owl perched on a branch above her head. He was peering down through his large dark eyes. Her heart began to pound even faster. She had known of a few Chihuahuas who were taken by owls.

"Why do you want to help us?" she called.

"I've never seen the likes of you little dogs in the forest," the owl hooted. "But you should know that two gray wolves are on your trail, and I must inform you that they would gladly eat you in a second."

Gray wolves! Lola could not take any more bad news.

Crack! Kaboom! The dogs yelped.

"Thunder and lightning—storm's on its way," the owl hooted.

"Where can we hide?" Lola asked, desperate, knowing she had no choice but to trust the owl.

"Tree next to mine got hit by lightning a while back, got a hollowed trunk. A family of cottontail rabbits lived there for some time, but they left a few days ago." Owl ruffled his feathers. "Kind of miss the little guys. Crawl through that crack in the tree trunk and don't make a sound."

"Joaquín, bring the dogs here," Lola barked. The dogs were all cowering on the ground, but Joaquín pushed them with his nose and his barking, "Get up, get moving!"

Kaboom! The dogs jumped up and ran to Lola, who ushered them through the crack in the tree trunk.

I hope nobody else is already in there, Lola thought as Clarita squeezed through.

But Clarita did not say a word once she disappeared into the trunk. Bambi went next. Nini. Manny, Pedro, and Pepe had to really squeeze, as did Mela, Bombom, and Joaquín.

Lola barely made it through the tree's narrow portal but she wiggled her way in and found herself in a completely dark but warm little space, where all the dogs nestled together, almost sitting on top of one another.

"That owl may have saved us," Lola said with great relief.

"Manny's sitting on my tail," Clarita started complaining, but before she said anything more. . .

Crack! Kaboom!

The dogs yelped even louder.

"Shhhhh," Lola whispered.

Lola peered out through the crack in the trunk into the black night and it was then that she saw two yellow glittering eyes. The yellow glittering eyes belonged to a gray wolf who stood beside the tree sniffing the ground.

"I smell something delicious," he said to another gray wolf standing close by. "Something delicious is in the tree. Almost smells like young Chihuahua, but I've never seen Chihuahuas in the forest. Could be rabbit."

The two gray wolves, their sleek muscles rippling upon their lean, rangy bodies, began casting their glittering glances in all directions.

"Must be up in the tree," the second wolf said, turning his yellow eyes up toward the branches.

Lola turned to the dogs huddled together in the dark, damp space, and with her anxious eyes she silently pleaded, *Don't say a word. Don't make a sound.*

The dogs stared back with wide eyes. Clarita's mouth began to open, but it quickly shut.

"That delicious smell is definitely coming from the tree," the second wolf said, bearing down on his haunches, then springing up into the tree and landing on a low branch.

The first wolf began pacing around the tree. In seconds, Lola knew, his glittering yellow eyes would find the crack. He would peer in and discover the ten Chihuahuas huddled together, trapped in the tree. Lola prayed the wolves would kill them swiftly and without too much terror.

Then, a terrible boom filled the air.

With the boom, a powerful jolt knocked Lola against the side of the trunk. The tree began to shake as if seized by a furious monster; it swayed side to side with such a force that all the dogs fell into a big pile. With Bombom, Mela, and Pedro now crushing her against the bottom of the tree trunk, Lola could feel the tree's roots beneath her creaking.

"What's going on," cried the second wolf, teetering on the branch.

"The tree is about to topple over," cried the first. "It's shaking as if possessed by *El Diablo*. But look around; only this tree is shaking. The other trees are still."

The tree began to split and the second wolf finally fell from the branch, hitting the ground with a thud.

"Yow," he howled. "That tree tried to kill me!"

No, Chili tried to kill you, Lola thought. The whirl of energy that shook the tree was the same force that kept the door from slamming in the hacienda. Chili had come to the rescue once again.

The first wolf growled, looking up at his friend. "Let's get out of here and go find a cave."

With great haste, the two gray wolves ran off.

Gracias, Chili, gracias, Lola thought as her pounding heart began to slow.

All night, the shivering Chihuahuas huddled together in the dark, damp tree trunk as the rain pounded and the wind howled and screamed. No one slept. No one spoke. It seemed as if the night would never end.

But the night finally did end, as did the rain and the wind. A misty light began to filter through the tree trunk's narrow crack, and the dogs lifted their soggy, exhausted heads and looked to Lola. She peered out into the forest and saw only quiet dawn.

"Come on," Lola said, and so the dogs squeezed back out of the hollow tree. For a few moments, the dogs walked about, stretching their legs and drinking from the puddles that had appeared everywhere.

Lola sat beneath the tree and looked at her wet and shivering dogs; their matted fur barely covered their skinny bodies. Bambi and Clarita had once been pampered pups, but now they both looked like drowning rats. Lola knew the dogs needed to find Pancho Villa and his cave of jerky soon or they would be too hungry and weak to travel any further.

"Let's go," Lola commanded, and she was relieved that all the dogs were still willing to follow her.

TWENTY-THREE

Though bravely trying to keep pace, Mela had fallen behind the pack. Bambi went back to see why she was struggling. What she saw made her gasp.

"Mela's paws are bleeding," Bambi told the others.

"It's okay, really, not so bad," said Mela with a wince, her face twisting in pain each time she set down her front paws.

The dogs stopped and gathered around Mela who began licking her paws, raw from walking so long over the sharp rocks, and stained red with blood. Lola's heart sank. Poor Mela was acting so brave but she could not walk anymore. They would have to stop. Lola looked over the side of the trail and she saw what looked like the entire world below. They were practically walking in the clouds.

"I'll look around and see if I can find a nice spot for Mela to rest," said Lola. "We'll need water. Perhaps there's a stream beyond those rocks. Joaquín, keep watch over the pack."

Lola trotted around the rock to the other side. By now, Lola recognized when a rock was really a cave, as the huge rocks so often were, and this rock appeared that it might be one. If it had an entrance, though, it was hidden, perhaps by the bramble that covered one side. Just then, Lola's nose went wild as a strong aroma hit her like a herd of galloping horses. Were animals living in the cave? Perhaps something had crawled in to die. Her sniffing nose soon uncovered an opening in the rock.

Lola stood before the opening and sniffed. Peewuh. Her nose went berserk, and, at the same time, her ears heard something rustling inside. Lola growled and the fur on her back rose. Her black whiskers started to twitch. Now she had done it—she had probably stumbled upon a sleeping gray wolf. This could be the cave the gray wolves escaped to last night. If a wolf came charging out, Mela with her wounded paws could never run away in time.

Maybe if Lola slithered away, the animal would return to sleep. Lola heard the rustling again. She turned and began running away from the cave when a rock bounced off her back.

That hurt! Angered by the attack, Lola spun around with a growl. A man was standing outside the cave, laughing. His hand raised over his head, he aimed a second pebble for Lola's head. She ducked just as it flew by.

"*Perrillo*, all alone?" A big smile spread across the man's wide face, which was brown as the dirt. A thick black moustache covered his mouth. His merry eyes crinkled all around the edges. Though it was still early morning, he was smoking a fat cigar, blowing perfect smoke rings into the air—one, two, three.

"Got some tequila, little Chichi?" the man asked mirthfully. "Waiting for my *compadres* but they won't come until tomorrow. Drank my last drop last night. Kills my pain."

The man clutched the knee of one leg and winced. Lola stared at the man and a funny feeling spread through her body.

"What you staring at, strange little rodent," the man bellowed. "Don't you know who I am?"

Lola felt as if the ground beneath her was falling away. The heavens opened above her.

"I'm the great Pancho Villa," the man continued. "Show your respect."

Lola stared at Pancho Villa standing before her, the man for whom she had almost sacrificed all her dogs. The man who she believed could save the Chihuahuas was wearing long underwear and a rumpled undershirt, both dotted with stains. He had thick black hair and a heavy black mustache that almost hid his entire mouth. A holster and gun were slung across his ample belly. He took another long puff from his fat cigar and this time blew four perfect smoke rings.

Pancho Villa. The hero of the Mexican Revolution was standing before her, looking as if he had just rolled out of bed, as if he had just rolled out of his cave. Laughing. Calling her little *perro*. Asking for tequila. In all the time Lola had imagined this moment, she had not known what she actually planned to do when she finally met Pancho Villa face-to-face.

"Ah, not alone," the man said.

Lola sensed her dogs behind her. Good, loyal dogs, they had heard the commotion and come to her side. She glanced over to see Bombom and Joaquín beside her. Nini, Pedro, Pepe, Manny, and Clarita stood close behind. Mela with her wounded paws was lying further back, Bambi hovering protectively.

The dogs stared at Pancho Villa, and Pancho Villa stared back, his eyes wide at the sight of the pack outside his cave.

"*Loco*, a pack of wild Chihuahuas way up here in the mountains?" he finally said, his voice deep and rough as the bark of the *mesquite*. He turned and spit on the ground. "I've seen wild dogs like you in the desert, but never up here in the mountains," he continued, wiping his mouth with his hand. "Did the *Presidente* send you to find me?" He slapped his leg with his hand and laughed, then winced at the pain. "Or maybe *El Gringo* Woodrow Wilson? I've heard he's looking for me too."

Just then a light went off in Bambi's head. "Is this the gentleman?" she asked, her little eyes narrowing. "The *Señor* we've been looking for?

Lola just nodded. Yes. Pancho Villa.

"Well, then," Bambi said, hotly, walking up until she was inches from Pancho Villa's huge, dusty bare feet. "I've got something to say to you, and you're going to listen! I didn't walk all the way up this mountain not to speak my mind. I didn't hide in a hollowed tree trunk while gray wolves paced around so that you could laugh at us. You, *Señor* Pancho Villa, or whatever you call yourself, have caused a lot of trouble in Mexico."

"Maybe you'd better not make this man too mad," said Mela, nervously standing behind Bambi.

"I will speak my mind," Bambi retorted. "You, *Señor* Villa, caused a lot of trouble in my *hacienda* and plenty of people are mad at you. *Señor* Terrazas, for instance, was absolutely livid. You should be ashamed for causing such pain to as nice a man as *Señor* Terrazas, not to mention the loss of our dresses in that fire and . . ."

Bambi went on talking a mile a minute, a streak of accusations that seemed to heat up the cool morning air by several degrees. Of course, all Pancho Villa heard was Bambi barking up a storm. Pancho Villa wasn't like *La Bruja*; he couldn't understand the dogs. Quick as a flash his mood switched from mirthful to maniacal.

"This *loco* little dog is making my blood boil," he shouted, waving his cigar in the air. "Shoo, get out of here, you wild dogs."

"Stop it," Lola barked at Bambi.

"My mother has a right to speak her mind," Clarita interjected, trotting over to Bambi's side. "It's a free mountain."

"Scram wild dogs," Pancho Villa said again, this time throwing the pebble in his hands. "Watch out or you'll be in my afternoon stew."

"Okay, we've found Pancho Villa. We'd better go now," said Manny, turning around and running away. Nini, Pepe, and Pedro were quickly on his heels.

"No," Lola barked. "We can't leave after coming all this way."

For what Lola saw before her kept her rooted to her spot. Here was Mexico's famous leader who had inspired people all throughout the north of Mexico to fight against the powers who wanted to keep them weak and poor, and now all Lola could see was a grumpy man with a sour temper.

Lola knew, more than ever, that she truly did have to help Pancho Villa.

So she continued sitting in her spot, gazing at the big ill-tempered man, his apple cheeks turning more and more red.

"Get out!" Pancho Villa shouted again, this time stomping his feet and waving his hands. "*Ay, caramba*," he shouted, jumping up and down on one foot. "That was my bad leg."

With that, Pancho Villa turned and shuffled back into his cave. If the cave had a door he surely would have slammed it.

"I guess we'd better go," Bombom said quietly. "He doesn't want us around. I guess the black serpents are now living in his brain. I don't know how we're going to help Pancho Villa, and how he's going to help us."

"At least the trip wasn't a total waste," said Mela, looking for the bright side. "We did bring Dolores to Josefina and José.

"You mean I have to walk all the way back down the mountain?" Clarita said, her eyes bulging and her tongue darting. "This trip was a total waste! I have a mind to go to Mexico City and call a meeting with *Presidente* Carranza, just as *Señor* Terrazas used to do when things didn't go his way. This Revolution has gone too far. But how will I get to Mexico City?"

"You won't go to Mexico City and this trip wasn't a waste," Lola said. "We can't give up this easily. We will sit here until Pancho Villa comes back out. Anyway, Mela can't walk anywhere until her paws heal."

"But what if he gets madder?" said Manny. "What if he really does make us into Chihuahua stew?"

"All I know is that we can't give up," Lola said with a heavy sigh. She lay down and rested her chin upon the ground, overwhelmed with exhaustion, for it had been a long journey indeed.

TWENTY-FOUR

The day passed slowly as the dogs lay together, so worn out from walking up the mountain and hiding in the tree trunk that they all took a long *siesta*, right in front of Pancho Villa's cave.

A heavy knocking woke Lola with a start. Her eyes flew open and she looked around. The sun had moved across the sky and the forest's shadows were lengthening yet again. Lola flashed on the gray wolves with their glittering yellow eyes. Perhaps the wolves were knocking about. Lola pricked up her ears believing she would hear them licking their chops.

But the knocking was coming from inside the cave. Maybe the gray wolves were inside, conspiring with Pancho Villa to make Chihuahua stew.

But at that moment Pancho Villa emerged from the cave, rubbing his eyes and yawning, as if he too had just awakened from a long sleep. His thick back hair was sticking up in all directions. A strange look crossed Pancho Villa's face when he saw the dogs.

"What are you little dogs still doing here?" Pancho Villa demanded in an outraged voice, tossing his *serape* over one shoulder and clutching it tightly against his chest. Bearing red, green, and white stripes, the *serape* looked like the Mexican flag, and for a quick second Lola remembered Bambi and Clarita's little dresses and felt a pang of regret that they had been completely ruined.

Maybe her quest had been ruined, just like the dresses.

"I thought I chased you away this morning," Pancho Villa continued. "Doesn't anyone listen to me anymore?"

"Maybe if you had better manners, they would," Bambi said haughtily, sitting up and stretching her neck.

A long moment passed while Pancho Villa glared at the dogs, now all awake and staring back.

"How did you all manage to climb up this mountain and not be eaten by the gray wolves?" he finally said. "I've never seen little desert dogs in the mountains. Not so many packs of wild Chihuahuas anymore, not like the old days when you ran through the desert by the hundreds. Used to run by the *hacienda* in Durango when I was just a boy, the Rancho de la Coyotada where I lived and worked with my family."

Pancho Villa wrapped his serape more tightly around his stout body and rapidly blinked his eyes.

Suddenly Pancho Villa did something that shocked Lola. He began to weep. Tears streamed down his apple cheeks, and he released big sobs into the cold dusk.

"The packs of wild Chihuahuas in Durango!" he exclaimed. "I used to run alone into the desert to get away from the *loco* noise of my brothers and sisters, and my mother and father always arguing about not having enough. Not enough food. Not enough *pesos*. Not enough shoes. Not enough *nada*. But the wild Chihuahuas running across the desert, aye *Mamacita*! I remember wishing I could be so free, to just run and run, away from the *hacienda* and from all of the work."

The dogs all stared at Pancho Villa as he cried.

"Pancho Villa isn't just a fierce, courageous leader," whispered Bombom. "He's a big baby too."

Pancho Villa's voice softened as he continued to talk. "I remember one particular day. It was my eleventh birthday but all my parents did was bicker about having *nada*. So I walked into the desert and waited until I saw the wild Chihuahuas coming."

Pancho Villa thrust his hands over his chest with great drama. "When I saw them running, jealousy clawed at my heart; I wanted the freedom of those little dogs," he said. "I wanted to hold a wild Chihuahua to see if I could somehow steal its free soul and keep it in my heart. All day, I tried to catch a little dog but they were too wily, too fast, too wild. I could never catch one."

Pancho Villa shook his great head back and forth as if to shake away the memory.

"Why do you taunt me, coming here and standing before my cave, to remind me of my failure? I told you to get out *muy rapido*, and now you mock me. Trapped in this cave, my bad leg throbbing with pain, eating nothing but *frijoles* and now no more tequila."

Pancho Villa put his hands on his hips. "My cousins are coming tomorrow with more supplies, but I'm sick of this mountain. I had to rest this bad leg, but now I'm done fighting. Going back to Chihuahua City and open a butcher shop. That's what I've always wanted to do."

The dogs around Lola cowered against the ground as the angry Pancho Villa waved his massive hands. "Scram," he yelled. Clarita and Mela buried their noses into their paws and whimpered.

But just as Pancho Villa's words blasted at the dogs, Lola was hit by a heavy aroma. The unmistakable smelly storm of salty sweat, leather, tobacco, and manure was coming up the mountain.

Man and horse.

Lola's ears pricked up to catch the sound of hooves digging into dirt and the sturdy smack of a leather whip against flesh. Yes, man and horse were coming near.

"What is it, Lola?" asked Joaquín, for he noticed her standing erect, her nose and ears alert. But before Lola could answer, Joaquín smelled the horses and man too, and he shot a look of pure alarm at Lola, his ears straight up and back. Lola and Joaquín locked eyes and exchanged the silent knowledge that they might have to save the dogs and Pancho Villa from this danger.

It occurred to Lola that these men and horses could be the *compadres* Pancho Villa had mentioned, the cousins bringing more tequila, but pure instinct told her that they were not. And in moments of real danger, pure instinct is all a dog has got. A dog knows to trust the anger in her gut, and her bristling fur.

Then Lola heard these singsong words: "Pancho Villa, Pancho Villa, come out, come out wherever you are."

Bursts of laughter punctuated the air.

"The sooner we find Pancho Villa, the sooner I can go home to Kansas City and eat a pile of barbeque ribs," one of the voices hollered.

"And peach pie," another voice added.

Lola knew these were in fact the white-faced American soldiers with their shiny black boots and shiny black guns, looking for Pancho Villa. The soldiers were a rock's throw away and it seemed certain they would find their catch in seconds.

Even though Pancho Villa was down on his luck, injured, and grumpy, Lola still had not had the chance to let Pancho Villa hold her, as he had held her father. She had not yet felt the pure power that flowed from his hands.

If the American soldiers captured Pancho Villa, she never would. Lola noticed all the color had drained from Pancho Villa's face and he was almost as white as the white-faced men. Almost, but not quite. He clutched the *serape* closer to his chest.

"Bombom, stay here with the pack," Lola barked, jumping from her spot and running around the rock with Joaquín right behind. Lola ran around Pancho Villa's rock to the clearing where the mountain trail began. It was here that Lola spied what had already filled her nose—three American soldiers on horseback coming down the trail. With shiny black boots and shiny black guns strapped to their waists, they cantered along at a fast clip.

Lola froze. What could the dogs possibly do to stop the soldiers from discovering Pancho Villa, and all the Chihuahuas for that matter? The soldiers were seconds from making the discovery.

"It's too late," Lola whispered to Joaquín, her voice quivering with dread. The horses were now practically upon them, kicking the dirt with their rapidly approaching hooves.

"No, Lola, it's not too late," Joaquín said. As Lola looked to Joaquín, she saw how his black eyes seemed to burn and spit out sparks from between his narrowed lids, and Lola remembered how those same spark flashed in his eyes that day in the desert when they had fought for control of the pack.

"Stay where you are and bark like crazy," Joaquín said. "Leave this to me!" And with that, Joaquín ran straight toward the men and horses unleashing a torrent of barks and howls.

"Whoa, Nelly!" one soldier yelled as Joaquín dashed right beneath the horses' hooves. "Was that some kind of rat? What the hell's going on?"

"Looked like some kind of stunted dog!" another soldier shouted back. "But he looks rabid!"

Indeed, Joaquín was barking with such intensity that his mouth foamed with spit. All the while, he jumped at the horses until they began bucking. Lola watched in horror as the horses' hooves kicked all around Joaquín's head. Still she barked, just as Joaquín had ordered her to do.

"That wild dog is going to scare our horses from here to Texas," the soldier yelled. "Shoot him, shoot him dead!"

One soldier fumbled for his gun but his horse was out of control and he could not quite grasp the handle.

Joaquín did not wait for the soldier to succeed; he tore down the trail, leaving a cloud of dust in his wake.

"Chase him, shoot him!" the first soldier yelled. "Kill that rabid dog!" And the soldiers took off after Joaquín, smacking their horses with their leather whips.

Suddenly, Lola was standing on the trail alone. She stopped in mid-bark and stared into the distance that had swallowed up Joaquín and the soldiers and the horses.

Several things happened to Lola then. First, her heart swelled with pride at Joaquín's fierce bravery. Joaquín could have been the pack's leader, Lola knew. Joaquín was smart and bold and was willing to give his life for the pack. But at the same time, Lola's heart ached with a wrenching pain because Joaquín was gone.

And at that moment, Lola felt as if her heart had broken into pieces, shattered by the sound of a gunshot that rang through the air.

TWENTY-FIVE

Lola stood on the trail and stared down the mountain. All was still. One of the soldiers must have shot Joaquín. Lola stared so hard down the mountain, looking for Joaquín, that black spots began to dance before her eyes. Then she noticed something strange. She squinted…was that a puppy, jumping and frolicking about? He reminded her of Joaquín when he was young, always teasing and taunting the other puppies with his endless energy. Lola blinked her eyes and squinted down the path again but the puppy was gone.

Frantic shouting pulled Lola back to the terrible present.

"*Qué pasó?*" shouted a wild, excited voice. "Those *Americanos* were looking for me, weren't they? I hid in the cave until I heard their horses galloping away. Who'd they shoot?"

Lola turned to see Pancho behind her, his big hands on his hips, his black eyes shiny with excitement. The *serape* he had clutched to his chest was gone and his stained shirt was now wet with sweat. The other dogs were on his heels, barking up a storm.

"What happened, Lola, did you scare away those men and horses?" barked Bombom.

"Was that a gunshot?" barked Manny.

Where's the other little *perro*," shouted Pancho Villa above the din of the dogs.

"Where is Joaquín?" Bambi barked. The dogs all stared at Lola with expectant faces.

Lola froze in fear at this terrible question, but before she could answer Pancho Villa knelt to one knee and began speaking in a hushed tone. "You chased away those *gringo* soldiers didn't you, little *perro*. You and the other brave *perro* chased them away. But why, when you could have run off with your pack?"

Pancho Villa put his hand to his heart. "Is it because you wanted to protect me?" he asked in an incredulous tone.

Lola stared at Pancho Villa. Had it been worth losing Joaquín to save Pancho Villa? If she could do it over, wouldn't she rather have Joaquín?

Still kneeling on one knee, Pancho Villa slapped his hand to his cheek. "I saw this once before, a pack of Chihuahuas barking just as fiercely to scare away *my* men," he said. "It was in the *pueblo* of El Apache a few years back. A pack of wild Chihuahuas came storming through. Their leader looked like you. He was in command of hundreds of Chihuahuas. I've never seen anything like it. Those dogs loved him. They surrounded my hut and barked and howled and bit my men's ankles because I'd trapped their leader. This was the Chihuahua I told you about earlier."

That Chihuahua had been Cuauhtémoc, Lola knew.

"As a boy I'd always wanted to hold a wild Chihuahua, so I trapped that dog under my *sombrero* and I took him in my hands."

Pancho Villa stared at his hands as if he could not believe his hands had done such a thing.

"I felt the raw power that flowed through that little dog's body. That Chihuahua inspired me to be a better leader. All these long years of the Revolution, especially in my darkest moments, I've thought of that wild Chihuahua and the way his dogs fought for him! I wanted my *campesinos* to be as strong and brave as those Chihuahuas and bite the ankles of the Mexican government as hard as they could too."

The other dogs stared up at Pancho Villa, then they turned their heads back toward Lola.

"Where is Joaquín?" said Bombom in a cold, frightened voice.

He's gone to be with Chili was all Lola could think to say, but before she opened her mouth, she heard, "Hey, everybody, I'm right here."

Lola spun around to see Joaquín coming up the mountain with a grin upon his face, his chest puffed out, looking as if it were the happiest day of his life.

"Joaquín!" the dogs all barked.

"The other *perro*!" Pancho Villa cried.

Lola rushed to Joaquín's side and licked his face. "I thought those white-faced men shot you," Lola said between licks.

Joaquín laughed. He howled. He began jumping and frolicking about the dogs, just as he had as a puppy.

"What fun! What excitement!" he barked. "To be chased by those horses and men. We Chihuahuas may be little but we're fearless and fast as the wind."

"But what about that gunshot, Joaquín? I thought the white-faced men shot you."

"One white-faced man shot himself in his own foot," Joaquín laughed. "The men and horses had chased me down the mountain, but when they caught up, I got under one horse and tried to bite his leg. You should have seen me, Lola! I was one *muy loco* Chihuahua. The *gringo* whipping his horse only made the scared animal buck harder. Suddenly, the gunshot, and all the horses began charging down the mountain with the men on their backs. Those *gringos* are surely in Tijuana by now."

Still kneeling on one knee, Pancho Villa stared at Lola and Joaquín with great interest. "If those *gringos* had come round the rock, they would have found me, and those *Americanos* would have delivered this Great Hero of the Revolution to *Presidente* Carranza and his *gringo amigo Presidente* Wilson. Little *perro*, come here." Pancho Villa held out his big hand. An odd feeling overcame Lola, and she thought of Maxi and how he would obey his master's orders.

Should Lola obey Pancho Villa? She froze in her spot.

"Go to Pancho Villa, Lola," Joaquín urged. "This is why you brought us up the mountain."

Lola inched closer to Pancho Villa's hand.

"Look how your dogs follow you," Pancho Villa said, for indeed every single dog had gathered around. Lola felt every dog encouraging her toward his hand.

"Was a time when my men would follow me straight into any danger, any battle, so loyal were they," Pancho Villa said.

Lola kept inching toward Pancho Villa, crouching to the ground and crawling toward his big, beckoning hand, until she was so close she could see right into his brown eyes that crinkled around the corners, his slightly turned-up nose, his skin wrinkled from the sun.

Now Lola would finally know how her father had felt when he was held by the great Pancho Villa. She too would feel the pure power that flowed from his hands. She put down her head and waited for the touch.

Just at that moment, though, a black crow flew over the dogs, cawing as it circled above Pancho Villa's head.

"*Loco* crow has been coming around the past few days," Pancho Villa grumbled as he shook his head and stood. "Sometimes I swear that crow is watching me."

Lola's heart sank. Now she would not know the touch of Pancho Villa's hand. But wait . . . a black crow? Lola stared into the sky. She stared at *La Bruja*, circling round and round, cawing. Suddenly the crow swooped down and cawed out a message for all the dogs to hear:

"Lola and Joaquín, by courageously working together and saving Pancho Villa, by getting those *gringos* off his trail, his heart is no longer pink with weakness and the black serpents have left his brain. You've shown Chili what brave leaders you truly are, and now Chili can finally cross over and become a star in the sky!"

Lola's heart lifted and seemed to break free from her body. It soared through the sky just like *La Bruja*, in pure happiness. The dogs all around were happy too and they barked and jumped.

As the merriment continued, Lola could swear that *La Bruja* had winked at her with her black crow eyes as her flapping wings lifted her higher and higher back up to the sky. Lola watched *La Bruja* fly so far away she seemed to just about brush the sun with her shiny black wings.

Cheered by the barking, howling, jumping dogs, Pancho Villa thrust his arms into the sky. "A *fiesta*!" he shouted, clapping his hands together overhead. "Come, you must be starving and thirsty. We'll have goat jerky and water. Yiyiyi, how I ache for my tequila, but we'll have a *fiesta* anyway."

The dogs remembered how famished and thirsty they were. Pancho Villa's goat jerky! Their mouths began to salivate.

Pancho Villa gave the dogs all his goat jerky, which turned out to be a big heap that tasted just as delicious as they had all imagined it would. As the dogs ate, Pancho Villa sat in the cave and sang *corridos*, his baritone voice bouncing off the walls as he sang ballad after ballad of lost love and found courage.

If Adelita would leave with another man
I'd follow her by land and sea
If by sea in a war ship
If by land in a military train.
If Adelita would like to be my wife
If Adelita would be my woman
I'd buy her a silk dress
To take her to the barrack's dance.

"The journey was stinkin' worth it," Pedro said, lying with the other dogs in a circle and chewing the salty treat.

"Pancho Villa's down on his luck, but who doesn't have a bad day now and then," said Pepe, smacking away.

"I'm glad we came to help Pancho Villa," added Nini, gobbling up another chunk of jerky from the pile. "I had my doubts a couple of times, especially hiding in that tree trunk, but look at us now, eating to our hearts' content."

"It was Lola who brought us here safely and kept the pack together," said Joaquín, his voice filled with gratitude.

"But you scared away the soldiers and saved Pancho Villa and the entire Mexican Revolution so that Chili could cross over and finally become a star," Lola said.

"No, Lola, we both did," Joaquín insisted with a shake of his head. "*La Bruja* said so and it's true."

Lola knew it was.

Bambi wrinkled her nose as she nibbled on her jerky. "I just hope by coming all this way to speak my mind I set a good example for my daughter. Remember, Clarita, you must always speak your mind in the face of adversity. We Chihuahuas may be small, but we don't take any nonsense from anyone."

"I won't forget, Mommy," said Clarita as she swallowed her own big mouthful of jerky.

That night, after all the other Chihuahuas had gone to sleep, Pancho Villa called Lola to his side in a corner of the dark cave.

"Special little *perro*, you sleep on my pillow," he said, patting the lumpy bag of hay. "Ay, who would have thought that both the Mexican and American governments would be searching for a poor boy from Durango, born to sharecroppers on the Rancho de la Coyotada."

Lola climbed onto the lumpy bag of hay.

"Times have been tough for us Mexicans during the last years fighting this Revolution," Pancho Villa said. He patted Lola's head. She didn't mind the pat. In fact, she liked it.

A rush of feelings overwhelmed Lola. Would she know now what her *padre* felt when he lay in Pancho Villa's hands all those years ago? Lola, her head down, rose from the lumpy pillow and walked to Pancho Villa's side. She looked straight into his hypnotic brown eyes.

Pancho Villa looked back into Lola's eyes, and then picked her up and held her in his strong hands, his rough and callused skin smelled like smoke, dirt, and goat jerky.

For several moments Lola waited to feel the power of Pancho Villa's strength seep through his hands into her fur. She waited and waited and finally a feeling came. But was it really Pancho Villa's power flowing through his hands that brought this wonderful mist of calm upon Lola?

Or was it simply the touch of a human? Was this feeling that filled Lola the reason that Maxi loved his master and stayed loyally by his side?

"Just like that other dog who came into my tent in El Apache, you are a fierce and courageous leader," Pancho Villa said, still cradling Lola in his strong hands. "I didn't think I wanted to go back to fight again, but now that you are here, I realize I can't turn my back on my people. If you, little *perro,* can protect your pack, I can protect my *campesinos*. Because of you, I'm going back down the mountain to fight once again for the people of Mexico."

FOUR MONTHS LATER

The journey down the Sierra Madre Mountains was quick and uneventful compared to the journey up. Pancho Villa's men packed the ten dogs into their saddlebags, laughing and teasing Villa the whole time about his little band of *Villistas*. The dogs went straight from the Sierra Madre Mountains down to Pancho Villa's ranch, which lay just outside Chihuahua City. Here the dogs had the run of the land.

Lola, Joaquín, Bombom, Nini, Pedro, Pepe, and Manny spent their days roaming the vast land, visiting the pigs and cows in the barnyard, and running after the horses. No more did they have to search for food and water as the ranch hands would place bowls of leftover *lengua* or *pollo* or *carne asada* inside the barn, where they would sleep each night in beds of hay.

Lola and Joaquín became particularly close and they would spend long hours talking about their puppyhood and the many adventures they had had in the desert. They wondered if any more wild Chihuahuas roamed through the desert or if, as Josefina had said, they had indeed been the last remaining pack.

Joaquín became the best friend Lola had ever known.

Sometimes the other ranch dogs would ask Lola and Joaquín to tell them stories about their lives as wild Chihuahuas. These farm dogs looked at them with big eyes, hungry for tales of the adventures they must have had running as far and wide as they wanted without man telling them to come back. Joaquín was especially good at spinning tall tales about fighting coyotes and gray wolves, holding the dogs captive with his outrageous stories, but Joaquín never revealed the truly unbelievable story of the dogs escaping the burning *hacienda* or meeting Josefina and *La Bruja*. They never talked about hiding in the tree trunk that long, stormy night. Joaquín kept those memories for Lola and himself.

Many days Lola would go inside the house to visit with Bambi, Clarita, and Mela, who had been adopted by the ranch foreman's wife and daughter. The lady dogs could keep Lola entertained for hours as they gossiped about the house cats and displayed their newest dresses.

Indeed, it was the daughter who took it upon herself to outfit these three dogs in clothes she had made herself. She gave Mela not a green velvet dress as Clarita had hoped, but a lovely pink cotton dress she had made from an old dinner napkin.

Bambi and Clarita, however, had the most stunning dresses, fashioned from a red and black silky fringed shawl that one of Pancho Villa's many dinner guests, a glamorous and famous singer from Veracruz, had left behind one night.

The numerous guests that came by when Pancho Villa was home, when he stole away to his ranch for a day or two of rest after weeks away, fighting and pushing on with the Revolution.

Lola never again saw the tired, grumpy man she had met on the mountain. That Pancho Villa had completely disappeared, replaced by the strong, confident leader who fearlessly led his revolutionaries to fight one battle after another.

"The man hated by thousands but loved by millions," Lola heard one guest say.

Mostly Pancho Villa was off fighting, however, and life on the ranch rolled along without him. But when enough time had passed, Lola would find herself sitting by the ranch gate, waiting and looking for Pancho Villa to return, galloping on his horse and shouting out his arrival.

Sometimes Lola would wait for days until she saw the spec of his horse on the horizon. She would stare for hours as the horse moved across the dry landscape, rejoicing when she finally recognized Pancho Villa's *sombrero* against the vast blue sky. Her heart would quicken in anticipation of the great leader's return. And with this quickening heart, Lola would always remember Maxi, the first dog to tell her of the joys of having a master, even though Pancho Villa was not her master but her *compadre*.

After Pancho Villa made his grand entrance and the entire ranch staff—the maids and cook and *vaqueros*—was upended by his requests and orders, he would finally pick up Lola and place her in his lap, calling her his little leader and saying she was the smartest, bravest Chihuahua he had ever met.

On one such evening, Lola was settled in Pancho Villa's lap as he lounged on his veranda, smoking his cigar, and he said, "Aye, *perrillo*, six years now we're fighting so my *campesinos* can keep their land, their dignity. We're weary and death has been our constant companion. But the people of Mexico don't give up. We draw our strength from the despair in which we have been forced to live."

Pancho Villa placed his hand on Lola's head. "There's no turning back and we will win because ours is a revolution of heart and mind," said, looking out across the vast desert. "I love this land. I love Mexico."

Then Pancho Villa became quiet and in the stillness Lola thought of Josefina's puppies that were surely getting bigger by the day, and of Dolores telling them all about the Techichis and the Aztecs.

Feeling as happy as she ever imagined she could, Lola looked upward into the clear black sky that was filled with twinkling stars. It was on this special night that Lola suddenly noticed two particular stars clustered close together and twinkling with a brightness that made her blink.

In that perfect moment, sitting on Pancho Villa's lap, Lola knew that Chili had indeed safely crossed over from the world of people and dogs into the sky where all the dogs that had lived in Mexico since time began and had run through the desert and over the mountains finally made their way to the stars.

As for the other star, for the first time Lola knew exactly whose star that was too.

Lola knew with all her heart that Chili would twinkle for infinity, as long as stars lived in the sky, and he would twinkle right alongside his dear old friend Cuauhtémoc.

THE END

Glossary of Spanish Words and Phrases in this Book

Abuela - Grandmother

Abuelo - Grandfather

Adiós - Goodbye

Ay, caramba - Oh My Gosh

Bruja - Witch

Campesino - Peasant, Farmhand

Carne Asada - Roasted Meat

Compadre - Friend

Corrido - Ballad

Diablo - Devil

Estúpido - Stupid

Federales - Federal Army

Fiesta - Party

Gringo - North American

Hacendado - Hacienda Owner

Hacienda - Large Estate

Hombre - Man

Jalapeño - Pepper

Lechuguilla - Little Lettuce

Lengua - Tongue

Libertad - Freedom

Loco - Crazy

Machete - Knife

Madre - Mother

Muchas Gracias - Thank You Very Much

Nada - Nothing

Padre - Father

Patrón - Boss

Perro - Dog

Perrillo - Little Dog

Peso - Mexican Coin

Pollo - Chicken

Pobre - Poor

Presidente - President

Pueblo - Village

Quinta - Country House

Señora - Mrs.

Señor - Mister

Serape - Colorful Shawl

Siesta - Nap

Sombrero - Hat

Tía - Aunt

Tierra - Land

Vaquero - Cowboy

Viva - Live Long

Zócalo - Main Square

About the Author

Traude Gomez Rhine lives in Pasadena, California, with her daughter, Ramona; husband, Michael; and their Chihuahuas.

Find out more about her work at Traudegomezrhine.com

Photo: Ramona Gomez

Acknowledgments

This book came to life through the support and guidance of my fabulous writing group and our extraordinary leader, Linzi Glass. Thank you, Ramona and Michael, for your everlasting love; Tody, for reading and encouraging early manuscripts; and to my mother, for always believing in my writing. I am grateful to Hortensia Chu and to Nola Butler for their professional guidance.

This story was inspired by many wonderful Chihuahuas, including Lola, Mela, Bambi, Clarita, Sofie, Bennie, Radcliff, and, of course, Daisy, the original Chihuahua, who channeled this tale to me during late-night writing sessions.

I am in perpetual awe of dog rescuers who are in the trenches every day, giving forgotten dogs a second chance at life and love.

You can support the important work of dog rescue at theforgottendog.org

Made in the USA
Monee, IL
05 February 2022